"I will *not* be s ... was terrified t ... would crumble her precious defenses.... He already had so much control—too much control. If he had *her*, then he would have it all.

He shrugged. "We both know if I started kissing you that I could have you on the bed in the back of this cabin within minutes. But with respect to our daughter I'll desist from making my point here and now."

All about the author…
Abby Green

ABBY GREEN deferred doing a social anthropology degree to work freelance as an assistant director in the film & TV industry—which is a social study in itself! Since then it's been early starts, long hours and mucky fields, ugly car parks and wet-weather gear—especially working in Ireland.

She has no bona fide qualifications but could probably help negotiate a peace agreement between two warring countries after years of dealing with recalcitrant actors. She discovered a guide to writing romance one day, and decided to capitalize on her longtime love for Harlequin® romances and attempt to follow in the footsteps of such authors as Kate Walker and Penny Jordan. She's enjoying the excuse to be paid to sit inside, away from the elements. She lives in Dublin and hopes that you will enjoy her stories. You can email her at abbygreen3@yahoo.co.uk.

Abby Green

IN CHRISTOFIDES' KEEPING

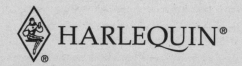

HARLEQUIN®

TORONTO • NEW YORK • LONDON
AMSTERDAM • PARIS • SYDNEY • HAMBURG
STOCKHOLM • ATHENS • TOKYO • MILAN • MADRID
PRAGUE • WARSAW • BUDAPEST • AUCKLAND

Recycling programs
for this product may
not exist in your area.

ISBN-13: 978-0-373-23743-2

IN CHRISTOFIDES' KEEPING

First North American Publication 2011

Copyright © 2010 by Abby Green

All rights reserved. Except for use in any review, the reproduction or utilization of this work in whole or in part in any form by any electronic, mechanical or other means, now known or hereafter invented, including xerography, photocopying and recording, or in any information storage or retrieval system, is forbidden without the written permission of the publisher, Harlequin Enterprises Limited, 225 Duncan Mill Road, Don Mills, Ontario, Canada M3B 3K9.

This is a work of fiction. Names, characters, places and incidents are either the product of the author's imagination or are used fictitiously, and any resemblance to actual persons, living or dead, business establishments, events or locales is entirely coincidental.

This edition published by arrangement with Harlequin Books S.A.

For questions and comments about the quality of this book please contact us at Customer_eCare@Harlequin.ca.

® and TM are trademarks of the publisher. Trademarks indicated with ® are registered in the United States Patent and Trademark Office, the Canadian Trade Marks Office and in other countries.

www.eHarlequin.com

Printed in U.S.A.

IN CHRISTOFIDES' KEEPING

This is for Lindi Loo and Lola,
my two favorite girls.

CHAPTER ONE

RICO CHRISTOFIDES stifled his irritation and tried to rein in his wandering attention. *What* was wrong with him? He was in one of the most exclusive restaurants in London, dining with one of the most beautiful women in the world. But it was as if someone had turned the sound down and all he could hear was the steady thump-thump of his heart.

He saw Elena gesticulating and speaking with a little too much animation, her eyes glittering a little too brightly as she tossed her luxurious mane of red hair over one shoulder, leaving the other one bare. It was meant to entice but it didn't.

He knew all the moves. He'd seen countless women perform them for years, and he'd enjoyed them. But right now he felt no more desire for this woman than he would for an inanimate wooden object. He regretted the impulse he'd acted on to call her up once he'd known he'd be in London for a few days.

Curiously, he was being enticed by a tantalising memory. He'd glanced fleetingly at one of the waitresses as they'd walked in and in an instant something about the way she moved had registered on his brain, throwing him back in time—two years back in time, to be precise. He'd found himself thinking of the one woman who hadn't been like all the others. The one woman who had managed to smash through the high wall of defences he kept rigid around himself and his emotions.

For just one night.

His fist clenched on his thigh under the table. It had to be just because he was back in London for the first time since that night. He forced himself to smile tightly in answer to something Elena had said, which seemed to require that response, and to his relief he could see that she was off again, clearly loving the sound of her voice more than she cared if he was listening or not.

The night he'd met *her*—*Gypsy*...if that even was her name—they'd just come out of the club and he'd been about to tell her his name. She'd put a hand over his mouth, saying fervently, 'I don't want to know who you are...tonight isn't about that.'

Scepticism hadn't been far away. Either she knew damn well who he was, as he'd been splashed all over the tabloids for days before that night, or else... But Rico had found himself pausing as he'd looked down at her. She'd looked so lovely and young and fresh...and untainted. And for that moment, for the first time in his life, he'd pushed aside cynicism and suspicion—his constant companions—and said, 'OK, then, temptress...what about just first names?'

Before she could say anything and still believing deep down and with not a little arrogance that she *had* to know who he was, he'd held out his hand and said with a flourish, 'Rico...at your service.'

She'd placed her small soft hand in his and hesitated for a long moment before saying huskily, 'I'm Gypsy.'

A made-up name. It had to be. He'd chuckled, and he could remember even now how alien it had felt to allow that emotion to rise up. 'Fair enough. Play your silly game if you want... Right now I'm interested in a lot more than your name...'

Someone laughed raucously at a nearby table, jerking Rico out of the memory, but even so a hot spiral of desire ran through him and he had a sudden memory flash of hearts beating in unison, sweat-slicked skin, her sleek body around his in an embrace so velvet hot and tight that he'd fought just to keep control. And then her muscles had started to spasm around him, she'd given a fractured breathy moan, and he'd lost it in a way that he'd never lost it before or since.

'Rico, *darling*...' Elena was pouting at him, lips too blood-red. 'You're miles away. Please tell me you're not thinking of boring work.'

Rico stifled a cynical grimace. It was that very *boring work*, and all the many millions he'd made in the process, that had women like Elena hovering around him in droves, waiting for little more than a crooked finger to signal his interest. Even so, the acknowledgement couldn't stop him from shifting uncomfortably in his seat, very disturbed by the fact that he was being turned on not by the woman opposite him, but by a ghost from the past. Because that ghost was the one woman who hadn't fallen at his feet in sycophantic ecstasy when he'd singled her out.

On the contrary: she'd tried to walk away from him. And then the following morning she *had* walked away from him. But not before he'd left her on the bed, like a callow, unsophisticated youth. Regret burned him, and Rico didn't *do* regret.

He forced another tight smile and reached

across for Elena's far too available hand. She practically purred when he took it. He opened his mouth to offer some platitude as a waitress walked past their table, and he frowned when his body inexplicably reacted—tightening almost as if it sensed something his brain hadn't yet registered. He looked up; it was the waitress he'd noticed on the way in. The waitress who had sparked a veritable torrent of memories.

Was he going completely insane? An evocative scent lingered on the air in her wake. He tried to sound casual, and not as if he was afraid he was going crazy. He looked back to his date. 'What scent are you wearing?'

Elena's lips curled seductively as she offered Rico her wrist to smell. 'Poison…do you like?'

He bent his head, but even before he smelt the distinctive perfume he knew it was all wrong. Nausea clenched his belly. He looked up again, as if drawn helplessly, to see the back of the waitress. She was taking an order at a nearby table. That evocative scent reminded him of— Abruptly Elena pulled her hand from his with a barely disguised huffy sigh and stood from the table, smoothing a hand over one artfully cocked hip sheathed in silk.

'I'm going to go and powder my nose.

Hopefully by the time I get back you won't be so distracted.'

Rico disregarded the reproach in her voice and didn't watch her walk away. He was transfixed now by the slim back of the petite waitress just a few feet away. She had a neatly shaped figure— firm buttocks, defined by the close-fitting black skirt which hid her legs to the knee, and slender but shapely calves and tiny ankles. Feet in low-heeled black shoes. So far so unremarkable.

His gaze travelled back up, past the plain white shirt, with just a hint of the bra underneath, taking in her hair, which looked a dark honey-brown but which he guessed might be lighter in daylight. It was densely curled, tied back into a tight bun, but he could already imagine the wild corkscrew curls that would burst free. Almost exactly like— He shook his head again, cursing softly. *Why* was that memory so hauntingly vivid tonight?

The woman turned slightly then, before stopping to respond to something the man at the table was saying, and it was enough to give Rico a proper glimpse of her profile. A small straight nose, determined chin, and a lush mouth with the slightest hint of an overbite—which he remembered thinking an adorable imperfection in a world obsessed with perfection. Certainty slammed into him on the heels of that thought—it had to be *her. He wasn't going crazy.*

His breath stopped. Everything went into slow motion as she finally turned and faced him directly. She was looking down at her notepad, scribbling something, juggling the big menus under her arm as she walked closer, and before he knew what he was doing, with something that felt horrifyingly exultant rushing through him, Rico stood and grasped the woman's arm, stopping her in her tracks.

Gypsy didn't know what was happening at first. All she knew was that someone had a tight grip on her arm. She looked up with a retort on her lips—and fell into steely grey eyes.

And stopped breathing, stopped functioning.

She blinked. Words died in her mouth. *It couldn't be him.* She was dreaming—or it was a nightmare. She was certainly tired enough to be sleep-walking. But she could feel the colour draining from her face, the peripheral noise fading into the background.

She was looking into exactly the same colour eyes as— There her mind shut down. *It was him.* The man who had haunted her dreams for nearly two years. Rico Christofides. Half-Greek, half-

Argentinian, billionaire entrepreneur, a legend of his own making.

'It *is* you.' He spoke her thoughts out loud in his deep voice, and sent Gypsy's brain into a tailspin. Very distantly she was aware of a voice screaming at her to run, get away. Escape.

She shook her head, but it felt as if she was under water. Was she still standing? All she was aware of was the dark depths of those deep-set stormy grey eyes, boring into her all the way to her soul, his hand tight on her arm. Midnight-black hair, slightly crooked nose, dark brows, defined jaw... It was all so familiar to her—except her dreams hadn't done him justice. He was so tall, towering over her, his shoulders so broad that she couldn't see anything but him.

Absurdly through the shock came the hurt—*again*—that he'd wasted little time in walking away from her the next morning. Leaving just an abrupt note which had read: *The room is paid for. R.*

A pointed cough sounded nearby. He didn't move, and Gypsy couldn't look away. Her carefully constructed world was crumbling into pieces around her.

'Rico? Is something wrong with our order?'

A voice. A female voice. Confirming what Gypsy didn't want to know by saying his name out loud. She registered dimly that it must be the stunning red-haired woman she'd walked past and noticed just minutes before. She couldn't believe now that she'd passed him so blithely, with no hint of warning.

But he ignored the woman and said again faintly, 'It's you.'

Gypsy managed to shake her head and at the same time somehow miraculously extricate her arm from his long-fingered grasp. She prayed that she could speak and say something that made sense. Something that would get her out of this situation and away from him. After all, it had been one night—mere hours—how could someone like him possibly remember her? After the way he'd left, why would he *want* to remember her? How could this awful fiery awareness be snaking through her veins?

'I'm sorry. You must be confusing me with someone else.'

Gypsy left him standing there and went straight to the staff bathroom, seriously afraid that she might be sick. Taking deep breaths over the sink, she felt clammy and sweaty. And all that was going through her mind was the imperative need to run, get away.

Ever since she'd found out that she was pregnant after their cataclysmic night together she'd known that some day she would have to tell Rico Christofides that he had a daughter. *A fifteen-*

month-old daughter, with exactly the same colour eyes as her father. Gypsy felt nauseous again, but willed it down.

She could remember her terror at the prospect of becoming a mother, along with her instantly deep and abiding connection with the tiny baby growing within her. And with that had come the intense desire to protect her child. She'd seen how Rico Christofides dealt with women who dared to name him as the father of their child, and had had no desire to expose herself to that public humiliation. Even if she'd been certain that she could prove paternity.

Pregnant, and feeling extremely nervous and vulnerable at the daunting prospect of how Rico Christofides might react to the news, Gypsy had taken the difficult decision to have Lola on her own. She'd wanted to be in a strong and solvent position when she contacted him. Working as a waitress, albeit in an upmarket restaurant, was *not* the ideal situation for her to be in when dealing with someone as powerful as him.

Panic surged again. Gypsy didn't even see her own white face in the mirror. If she didn't get out of there *now*, Rico Christofides couldn't fail to recall the woman who had acted completely out of character and who, on a tide of desire so intense that she still woke sometimes at night *aching*, had succumbed to his masterful seduction and indulged in a one-night stand.

Making a fateful decision, uncomfortably aware that she was acting on blind instinct and panic but seeing no other solution, she splashed some water on her face and went to find her boss.

'Tom, please,' Gypsy begged, and mentally crossed everything. She hated lying, and especially using her daughter to do it. But she had no choice. Not with the father of her child just through the kitchen doors.

'I have to get home to Lola. Something has… come up.'

Her boss raked his hand through his short sandy hair. 'Jeez, Gypsy you really pick your moments—you know we're short staffed as it is. Can't it wait for another hour, until we have the main rush over with?'

Gypsy hated herself for this. She shook her head, already taking off her apron as she did so. 'I'm sorry, Tom. Really sorry—believe me.'

His face tightened and he crossed his arms. Gypsy felt the slither of fear trickle down her spine. 'So am I, Gypsy. I don't want to do this to you, but it's come to this: you've been late nearly every day for the past two weeks.'

Gypsy started to protest, saying something

about the inflexible hours of her daughter's minder conflicting with her shift hours, but her boss cut her off.

'You're a good worker, but there's a line of people behind you waiting to get a job here who won't let me down like this.'

He took a breath, and Gypsy's foreboding increased. 'If you leave like this now then I'm afraid you won't have a job to come back to. It's that simple.'

A vivid memory surged back of the moment she'd found out that the man who had turned her world upside down was none other than one of the world's most powerful men, and nausea returned.

The thought of going back out to the dining room and trying to function normally was inconceivable. She'd end up getting fired anyway for spilling someone's dinner into their lap, she was shaking so much. She looked at Tom and shook her head again sadly, already anticipating the drudge of having to look for another job, silently giving thanks that she had some savings to tide them over for a couple of weeks. 'I'm sorry, Tom, I have no choice.'

Her boss stood back after a long moment and gestured with his arm. 'Then I'm sorry too, Gypsy, because you're leaving *me* no choice.'

She couldn't say anything. Her throat was

too tight. She gathered up her things and left through the back kitchen door, stepping out into the dark and dank alleyway behind the exclusive restaurant.

Later that night Rico stood at the floor-to-ceiling window of his central London penthouse apartment, hands dug deep into his pockets. His pulse was still racing, and it had nothing to do with the beautiful woman he'd said a curt and sterile goodnight to—much to her obvious disgust—and everything to do with a pretty waitress who had confounded him by doing a disappearing act.

She'd done a disappearing act the first time round, but he only had himself to blame for that. He grimaced; if he hadn't panicked… It still rankled with him that he'd let her get under his guard so easily. He could remember watching her sleeping, sprawled across the bed, feeling seriously stunned at the depth of his desire, *still*, and the depth of his response to her.

It was that and the overwhelming feeling of possessiveness which had driven him from the room as if hounds were snapping at this heels. He *never* felt possessive of women. But this evening, the minute he'd recognised her, it had surged upwards again, as fresh as if no time had passed. And she'd run. And he had no idea why.

He pulled out a small piece of paper from his pocket. He'd got her name from the manager of the restaurant, and his men had made short work of tracking her down. He now had Gypsy Butler's address—for apparently that *was* her name. He smiled grimly. He would soon find out what exactly he found so compelling about a woman he'd slept with for just one night, and why on earth she'd felt the need to run from him.

The following morning, as Gypsy walked home in drizzly rain from the local budget supermarket, pushing a sleeping Lola in her battered buggy, she was still reeling at what had happened the previous evening.

She'd seen Rico Christofides and she'd lost her job.

The two things she'd been most terrified of happening had happened in quick succession. She defended herself again: she'd had no choice but to leave last night—she'd have been in no fit state to work or deal with Rico Christofides. Her legs felt momentarily weak when she recalled how he'd looked, and how instantaneous his effect on her had been.

He'd been tall and strong and devastatingly

powerful. And still as bone-meltingly gorgeous as the first time she'd seen him across that crowded nightclub two years ago.

The night she'd met Rico had been a moment out of time—and most definitely a moment out of character. He'd caught her on the cusp of her new life, when she'd been letting go of a lot of pain. She'd been vulnerable and easy prey to the practised charm of someone like Rico Christofides. But she'd had no clue then just exactly who he was. A world-renowned tycoon and playboy.

Seeing him had made everything she'd ever known pale into insignificance. She knew if he'd been dressed like the other men in the club—in a natty shirt and blazer, pressed chinos—it would have been easy to dismiss him as being like all the rest. But he hadn't been dressed like that. He'd been dressed in a T-shirt and faded denims which had fit lean hips and powerful legs so lovingly that it had been almost indecent. An air of dangerous sexuality had clung to his devastatingly dark good-looks in a way that had left everyone around him looking anaemic—and awestruck.

But that in itself would have just made him a spectacularly handsome guy; it had been more than that. It had been in the intensity of his gaze across that heaving chaotic club—*on her*. Dark and mesmerising, stopping Gypsy right where she'd been dancing alone on the dance floor.

The impulse to get out of her tangled head and engage in something physical had called to her as she'd passed the club doors and heard the heavy bass beat just a short while before. It was a primal celebration of the fact that she was finally free of her late father and his corrupt and controlling legacy. When he'd died six months previously she'd felt more emptiness than grief for the man who had never shown her an ounce of genuine affection.

But when the gorgeous stranger had started to come towards her in the club, with singular intent, all tangled thoughts and memories had fled. He'd cleared an effortless path through the thronged crowd—and sanity had returned to Gypsy in a rush of panic. He was too handsome, too dark, too sexy...too much for someone like her. And the way he'd looked at her as he grew ever closer had scared the life out of her.

But, as if rooted to the spot by a magic spell, she hadn't been able to move, and had just watched, dry-mouthed, as he came to stop right in front of her. Tall and forbidding. No easy sexy smile to make it easier. It was almost as if something elemental had passed between them and this man was claiming her as *his*. Which had been a ridiculous thing to feel on a banal Friday night in a club in central London.

'Why have you stopped dancing?' he'd asked innocuously, his deep voice pitched to carry across the deafening beat, but even so she'd heard the unmistakably subtle accent.

He was foreign. As if his dark looks wouldn't have told her that anyway. A frisson of awareness had made her tremble all over when she'd noted his steely grey eyes, their colour stark against his olive skin. She'd shaken her head, as if to clear it of this madness, but just then someone had jostled her, heaving her forward and straight into the man's arms, into hands which held her protectively against his hard body.

Instantaneous heat had exploded throughout Gypsy's body at the sheer physicality of him. She'd looked up, utterly perplexed, and had sensed real fear... Not fear for her safety, but an irrational fear for her *sanity*. On a rising wave of panic she'd used her hands to push against his chest and stepped back, answering tightly, 'I was just leaving, actually...'

His big hands had tightened on her arms— bare because she was wearing a sleeveless vest. Her light jacket was tied about her waist, her bag slung across her chest. 'You just got here.'

He'd been watching her from the moment she'd arrived. Gypsy had felt weakness pervade her limbs to think of how she'd been dancing: as if no one was watching.

And then he'd said, 'If you insist on leaving, then I'm coming with you.'

Gypsy had gasped at his cool and arrogant nerve. 'But you can't—you don't even know me.'

His jaw had been hard and implacable. Stern. 'Then dance with me and I'll let you go...' The fact that he hadn't been cajoling, hadn't been drunkenly flirting, had imbued his words with something too compelling to resist.

Gypsy's focus came back to grim and grey reality as she was forced to stop by the traffic lights. She didn't need to recall the pitifully pathetic attempt she'd put up to resist before agreeing—ostensibly to make him let her go.

But it had had completely the opposite effect. After dancing with her so closely that her body had been dewed with sweat and heat and lust, he'd bent low to whisper against her ear. 'Do you still want to leave alone?' To her ongoing shame and mortification, she'd shaken her head, slowly and fatefully, her eyes glued to his in some kind of sick fascination. She'd wanted him with a hunger the like of which she'd never experienced in her life.

She'd let him take her by the hand and lead her out of the club, seeing him as somehow symbolic of the cataclysmic events of the day that had just passed, during which she'd finally let go of everything that had bound her to her father.

She'd allowed herself to be seduced…and then summarily dumped like a piece of trash the following morning. She remembered seeing the curt note he'd left, and how cheap she'd felt—as if all that was missing was a bundle of cash on the dresser.

With an inarticulate sound of disgust at herself to be thinking of this *now*, the fact that she'd let a man like him—a powerful man *just like her father*—seduce her, Gypsy strode on across the road once the traffic had stopped. With any luck Rico Christofides would have become distracted by the vision of perfection he'd been dining with last night and forgotten all about her. *But he remembered you…* She realised that any other woman would be feeling an intensely feminine satisfaction that a man like him hadn't forgotten her, but *she* just felt panicky. *Why* on earth did a man like him remember someone like her?

A familiar sense of despair gripped Gypsy as she turned into her road, full of boarded-up houses and disaffected-looking youths loitering on steps. As much as she'd relished her freedom after her father's death, and as much as she wouldn't have minded living somewhere like this if she'd only had herself to worry about, it did bother her that her daughter's first home was in such a decrepit part of London. Even the nearby children's playground was vandalised beyond use, with just one pathetic swing left.

She sighed heavily, very aware of the irony that, but for her hot-headedness and determination to dissociate herself from her father, she might have been living in much more upmarket surroundings. But then she knew she could never have lived off her father's money—and she'd never have dreamed that she'd become pregnant after a one-night stand with a ruthlessly seductive—

Gypsy's heart stopped stone-cold dead in her chest—and it had nothing to do with the faintly menacing-looking youths crowded around the steps of a nearby house and everything to do with the stunning car they were eyeing up.

The gleaming black luxury vehicle with tinted windows should have belonged to one of the gangsters that had a stranglehold on the area, but Gypsy knew immediately it was a world apart from their cars. The gangsters around here could only *wish* to own a car like this.

And as she drew closer, and saw the back door swing open, her heart picked up speed, so that it was nearly leaping from her chest as she watched a tall, dark and powerfully built figure uncoil like a panther stretching lazily in the sun.

As if she didn't already know who it was, he turned to face her. Just feet away, and right outside her front door. No escape.

Rico Christofides.

CHAPTER TWO

GYPSY knew she couldn't run. The very thought was futile—as evidenced by Rico Christofides' clear determination to find her. *Why* was he so intent? All Gypsy had to do was picture the woman from last night and the contrast between them was laughable.

Today she was in her habitual uniform of too baggy jeans bought from a local charity shop, layers of threadbare jumpers to block out the January cold, sneakers, a secondhand parka and a woolly hat pulled down low over her ears and too wild hair. *He*, on the other hand, looked every inch the successful tycoon, in a long, black and expensive-looking coat, with the hint of a pristine suit underneath.

She saw his slaty grey eyes narrow on her as she approached. No doubt he was regretting his impetuous decision to find her. And then her skin prickled as she saw his gaze drop to the pram she pushed, with a sleeping Lola inside, obscured by the rainshield.

His daughter—oh, God—could he know?

Gypsy immediately reassured herself there was no way he could know. Why would he assume for a second that Lola was his? She just had to take advantage of the undoubted regret he'd already be feeling at seeking her out and get rid of him. As soon as possible—before he could see Lola and guess.

Even if he didn't guess she knew that once she told him about Lola he'd move heaven and earth to prove that she wasn't his—which was what she'd seen him do before. And then, when paternity was proved, he'd set out to control his daughter utterly. Exactly as her father had done to her once *he'd* had no choice but to accept her.

She knew this because Rico came from her father's world of powerful men who thrived on being ruthless. Men who dominated those around them.

As soon as she'd heard his name she hadn't been able to believe she hadn't recognised him. She even recalled overhearing her father speaking bitterly of Rico Christofides on more than one occasion: *'If you think I'm ruthless then don't ever cross Rico Christofides. The man is a cold machine. If I could beat him I would, but*

*the bastard wouldn't rest until he'd resurrected
himself from the dead and ruined me in the process. Some fights just aren't worth it, but I'd give
anything to see his arrogance smashed...'*

Her father had been obsessive, and the
memory of that almost grudging admiration had
blasted away any chance that she might have
contacted Rico Christofides before today.

The best that Gypsy could hope for was that
that day wasn't going to be today, and that perhaps she could escape with Lola—go somewhere new, away from London—until such time
as she could get her wits about her again and
decide what was best for them both.

She was glad now of her plain and dowdy
appearance. Rico Christofides must already be
forming some escape route of his own. She'd
help him along, agree with him that he must
have the wrong person, and then he'd get back
into his luxury car and be off, out of her life,
until such time as she invited him back in, when
she was ready to deal with him. With that assurance, she steeled herself and walked forward.

Rico watched the woman come towards him.
For a second he faltered. Was this *her*? The
woman approaching slowly looked impossibly plain from a distance, bare of any make-
up or artifice. Pale. And her body was all but

swamped in clothes that looked as if they'd just been dragged out of a skip.

And she had a child. Something which felt suspiciously like disappointment sent his brain reeling, and he clamped down on that emotion hard. A child was a complication. She came closer, and as he lifted his gaze back to her face he was already trying to come up with some excuse for having come all this way to find her, still doubting that it might be her. Perhaps he had been completely mistaken. Perhaps the name was a freak coincidence.

But then she drew closer, and all thoughts of children and complications fled as his body reacted with a helpless lurch of desire. It *was* her.

Despite her appearance, he could see the intensity of those huge green eyes now, framed with long black lashes, the delicate bone structure, her lush mouth. And her hair, with its irrepressible curls trailing out from under the tatty hat over her shoulders. It reminded him of the moment he'd first set eyes on her in that club. He'd been cursing himself for having gone at all, hating that he'd given in to weak restlessness, and then *she'd* walked in. Dressed in snug jeans and a vest top, completely at odds with the glitter of the too coiffed women who'd thronged the place. The expression on her face had been intense, as if she was being driven by inner demons, and it had resonated within Rico.

The firm swell of her breasts had been clearly outlined against the thin material of her top, and he'd watched, entranced, as she'd walked straight to the middle of the dance floor and started to dance with completely uninhibited grace. He'd seen plenty more beautiful women in his time, clothed and unclothed, but something about her lithe little figure, with its hint of sensual plumpness, had been more enticing than any gazelle-like beauty he'd ever known. With her tawny curly hair she'd looked wild, and free, and it had called to him on a base level too urgent to ignore...

She'd been exquisite. She *was* exquisite. Even though he could see at a glance now that she'd lost weight. Relief flooded him in a way that made him very nervous as she came to a standstill where he blocked the path. And along with the relief came irrational anger to find her living in such an obviously dangerous area. The anger surprised him; women didn't normally arouse feelings of protectiveness within him. He'd noted the local thugs with distaste after he'd knocked and got no answer from her door, and retreated to his car to wait. They'd tried to intimidate him, but after one quelling look they'd recognised the danger within him and maintained a respectful distance.

Right at that moment he'd completely forgotten that he'd just considered making his excuses and leaving. That was now the last thing on his mind.

Gypsy decided to pretend that she didn't know who he was, that she hadn't just seen him again last night. It was cowardly, she knew, but she was counting on him wanting to make his escape from someone who looked like a bag lady.

'Excuse me—you're blocking my way.'

He didn't move aside. Those penetrating grey eyes were fixed on her with unnerving intensity, and Gypsy could feel a flush of response rise up through her body as it reacted with dismaying helplessness to his proximity. As it was she was battling to keep back the images that threatened to burst free. Images of sweat-slicked bodies moving in desperate tandem, straining to reach the pinnacle...

'Why did you run last night?'

His deep voice cut through those disturbing images. Her lie fell out with an ease that would have had her horrorstruck in any normal circumstance. 'My daughter...I had to get home to my daughter.' And then she cursed herself. She hadn't denied that she'd *run*.

At that moment the rain started to fall more heavily, scattering the local teens around them. Rico Christofides gestured to her door, which was up a few steps. 'Let me help you with the pram.'

Panic rose. Gypsy protested, not wanting him anywhere near her place or Lola. 'No, really, I can manage…' But even as she spoke Rico Christofides took hold of the pram and lifted it bodily against him, as if it weighed no more than a bag of sugar. She had to let go or it would have become a tug of war. The irony that Lola could become an object of a tug of war was not lost on Gypsy at that moment.

The rain was teeming down now, flattening his black hair against his skull. Gypsy could feel drops of water falling down her back. When he gestured with his head, she had no choice but to precede him up the steps to the front door. In the manoeuvring that was done to open the door and get Lola inside, with Rico Christofides hanging onto the buggy relentlessly, he was in her tiny one-bedroomed apartment before she knew what was happening or could stop it.

He placed the buggy back down in the pitiful excuse for a sitting room with a gentleness that momentarily disarmed Gypsy. She was a little stunned. With a brusque economy of movement he shut the main front door and came back to shut her ground-floor apartment door. Now he was looking around, and asked, 'Have you got a towel?'

'A towel?' Gypsy repeated stupidly, knowing on some level that she was going into shock.

'Yes,' he said slowly. 'A towel… You're soaked through and so am I.'

'A towel,' she repeated again, and then, as if jolted by a stun gun, she came out of her shocked inertia. 'A towel—of course.' *Get the towel, let him dry off and he'll be gone.*

Gypsy walked on stiff legs to the tiny bedroom she shared with Lola and opened the cupboard to take out a towel. Coming back, she handed it to Rico Christofides, trying not to notice how huge he appeared to be in the small room.

Immediately he frowned and handed the towel back to her. 'You first—you're soaked. Surely you have more than one?'

Gypsy looked at it stupidly, and then gabbled, 'Of course.' She gestured jerkily. 'You take that one. I'll get another.' She tried not to let the mounting impatience she felt be heard in her voice. Why wouldn't he just *leave*?

Coming back to the sitting room, she saw him drying his hair roughly with big hands. He'd taken off his coat to drape it over a threadbare chair, and his impeccable suit was moulded to his strong frame, making her throat dry at recalling the body underneath.

He turned to face her, taking his hands down, leaving his short hair sexily dishevelled. He glowed with vitality and health, making Gypsy feel pale and wan.

He frowned down at her. 'You should take off your coat and hat...' He looked around. 'Do you have a heater in here?'

Reluctantly she pulled off her hat and started to undo her coat, knowing he was right; the last thing she needed was to get ill. She shook her head when those grey eyes settled on her again, expecting an answer, and flushed when they dropped imperceptibly to take in her shabby clothes as her coat slid off. She was very aware of her hair, which now curled in wild abandon around her shoulders, and could just imagine how frizzy it would be from the rain. She wanted to pull it back and tie it up. And she hated that he was making her aware of herself like that.

'Our heater broke this morning. The storage heating will come on in a couple of hours.'

Rico Christofides looked comically shocked. 'You've no *heat*? But you have a child—it's freezing outside.'

Gypsy flushed with a mother's guilt. 'This is the first day it's been broken. We'll manage until we can get a replacement...' She trailed off, suddenly thinking of the fact that now she was out of work her meagre savings wouldn't be stretching to cover a new heater. As if she could explain she'd lost her job because of him. How irresponsible was she?

She looked at Rico Christofides and recognised his wide-legged stance with dismay. He wasn't going anywhere any time soon. With extreme reluctance she finally said, 'Can I get you tea or coffee?'

His eyes narrowed on her once again. The barest hint of a smile tipped up one corner of his wickedly sensual mouth as he recognised her capitulation. 'I'd love a coffee, please. Black, no sugar.'

Stark, with no sweetener—just like him, Gypsy thought churlishly as she went into the kitchen to put on the kettle. All she could hope for now was that Lola wouldn't wake up and Rico Christofides would satisfy whatever bizarre lingering curiosity he had about her and leave. Soon.

Rico looked around the bare apartment as Gypsy moved about the kitchen and he suppressed a shudder of distaste. Without her presence right in front of him his brain seemed to clear slightly. Once again he questioned his sanity in pursuing her here, especially when his eyes fell on the battered-looking buggy which sat just feet away against the wall. His sane impulse was to come up with some plausible excuse—even just ask her why she seemed to be determined to pretend she didn't know him—but a greater overriding impulse was urging him to stay. Even if there was a child in the picture.

He could only make out the fact that her daughter was quite small, so therefore she must have had her since she'd been with him. And even though Rico knew he had no right to feel a surge of anger at that, *he did*.

Even just watching her pull off that damned unflattering hat and coat had scrambled his brain and made him almost forget the presence of the child. The quick movement of her small hands had reminded him of how they'd felt on him, stroking along the most sensitive part of his anatomy until he'd had to beg her to stop... He frowned. *Why* was she so intent on denying she knew him? And that night? Even if he had left the way he had, he knew it had been as cataclysmic for her too. The shocked look of awe on her face just after she'd exploded around him had told him that.

With no false pride he knew he was a good lover, but what he'd experienced that night with Gypsy had gone beyond anything he'd ever known before. *Or since*. It had shaken him out of his complacency. Was that why he needed to see her again? To recapture that moment? To see if it had been his imagination or something… more? He balked at that. He never wanted anything *more* with any woman. But that night with Gypsy had touched him on a level that had left him feeling an ache of dissatisfaction, and it had only grown since then, pervading everything around him and tainting the few liaisons he'd had with women in the interim.

He knew seeing her last night had thrown the fact that he'd been trying to recapture that fleeting transcendence he'd experienced with her into sharp relief. With that thought reverberating through his mind he heard Gypsy re-enter the room. He turned to face her and took the coffee she held out. She was avoiding his eyes.

Gypsy escaped Rico's gaze and occupied herself by going to peek in at Lola who, to her relief, was still sleeping peacefully, her cheeks pink and her rosebud mouth in a little moue. Long black lashes rested against plump baby cheeks. Gypsy's heart swelled, as it did every time she looked at her daughter, and at that moment she felt an overwhelming surge of guilt at knowing she was denying Lola's father knowledge of her when he stood only feet away.

She quashed it down, telling herself that she was doing it for good reasons, and straightened up, crossing her arms defensively over her chest. To her surprise she saw that Rico Christofides had taken a saucepan from the kitchen and was placing it in the corner of the room where, to her dismay, she saw that he'd spotted a leak.

As he straightened up again she said, more caustically than she'd intended, 'Look, what is it you want from me?' The rogue thought that he could be there because after seeing her again he'd been overcome with lust set her mind spinning, before she realised how unlikely that had to be.

Rico Christofides calmly sat down on the two-seater sofa and indicated for Gypsy to sit down too. With a barely disguised huff, which was really more fear than impatience, she took the chair opposite the sofa. He took a lazy sip of coffee before putting the cup down on the chipped table.

'I'd like to know why you seem to be so determined to pretend we've never met, when in fact we're intimately acquainted.'

Gypsy blushed to the roots of her hair at the way he said *intimately*. Tightly, she answered, knowing it was futile to keep pretending otherwise. 'I am well aware of the fact that we've met before, but I've no desire to become reacquainted.'

He regarded her for an uncomfortably long moment and then said, 'You may not believe this, but I regretted leaving you the way I did that morning.'

A spasm of emotion made Gypsy clamp her lips together. She didn't doubt this was just a smooth move—he most likely hadn't given her a second thought. Perhaps he'd seen her last night and assumed she might be as easy to seduce again. 'Well, I don't. And you're forgetting that you left your kindly informative note.'

His face tightened. 'Contrary to what you might have thought after that night, I'm not in the habit of picking women up in clubs and booking into the nearest hotel for a night of anonymous sex.'

Gypsy burned inside, but shrugged nonchalantly. 'Look, what do I know or care? It's not something I gave much thought to.'

He sent a pointed look towards Lola's pram, and said ascerbically, 'Clearly I can see that perhaps one-night stands are a habit for you.'

Gypsy gasped in affront and sat up straight, hands clenched on her lap, 'How *dare* you? I'd never had a one-night stand in my life before I met you.'

He arched a brow. 'And yet,' he drawled easily,

'you were remarkably eager to throw yourself into the experience that night, *Gypsy Butler*.'

Gypsy's heart stopped. He knew her full name—of course he did; he'd found her. He'd be able to track her down no matter where she went now. They must have given it to him at the restaurant.

He asked now, 'So, that really *is* your name?'

Gypsy nodded, wanting him gone more than ever now, not liking the way he was making her feel so trapped, and said distractedly, 'My mother had an obsession with Gypsy Rose Lee, hence the name.' She left out the fact that for a good portion of her life she hadn't been called by her birth name at all. As far as she was concerned that part of her life had ended when her father had died.

Forcing her mind away from those memories she said, harshly but quietly, mindful of Lola, 'Look, what is it you want? I'm busy.'

He cast her a scathing glance. 'Busy trying to get away from me, for some reason.' His eyes narrowed on her, and she felt like a tiny piece of prey in front of a predator, with no escape in sight. 'And at high cost—especially when I happen to know that your disappearing act last night lost you your job...'

Gypsy held in a gasp but said shakily, 'How do you know that?'

His shoulder moved minutely, 'The waiters were remarkably indiscreet and loud.' Taking her by surprise, Rico Christofides asked then, as if it had just occurred to him, 'Where is your child's father?'

Sitting in front of me, she thought hysterically, and schooled her features, hitching up her chin in an unconscious gesture of defiance. 'We're alone.'

'You have no other family?'

Gypsy shook her head, and tried to ignore the feeling of vulnerability his words provoked. Rico Christofides was grim. 'Which proves my point, don't you think? You slept with me and at least one other man soon after—for I can't imagine that you had left a small baby in the care of a stranger while you were with me that night.'

Gypsy shook her head, aghast at the thought of leaving Lola like that while she went off to spend the night with someone. 'Of course I didn't. I would never have done something like that.'

Rico Christofides looked almost smug. She'd proved his point for him, albeit erroneously, because of course she hadn't slept with anyone else since him. With panic galvanising her movements, making them jerky, Gypsy stood up with clenched fists at her sides. 'Look, Mr

Christofides, you're really not welcome here. I'd like you to leave.'

It was only at his sharply drawn together brows and the way his head snapped up that Gypsy ran over what she'd just said and realised with sick horror its import.

He rose slowly and looked down at her, frowning, and Gypsy felt the horror spread through her when he said, 'You know who I am. So you *did* know who I was that night?'

She shook her head, feeling sick, the possible future implications of her knowledge too much to consider right now. 'No...no, I didn't. It was only the next morning...when I saw you on the news...'

It had been just after she'd read his note and realised he'd gone. She'd seen the TV in the corner of the room, on a news channel and on mute. He'd obviously been watching it before he'd left that morning. To her utter surprise she'd seen *him*, clean-shaven and pristine in a suit, looking almost like a different person, walking down the steps of an official building surrounded by photographers and an important-looking entourage. Gypsy had raised the sound and watched with mounting horror as she'd discovered exactly who Rico was.

'And yet you never contacted me once you knew...you still left...' He said this almost musingly, as if trying to work her out. Gypsy knew that in his world women who wouldn't take advantage of a one-night stand with a man like him would be few and far between.

She nodded her head vigorously. 'Yes, I left.' And then, far more defensively than she liked, 'I got the hint that morning when I woke and you were long gone, leaving a note which made me feel like a call girl, and to be perfectly honest I have no interest in discussing this any further. I'd like you to leave *now*. Please.'

At that moment, to Gypsy's utter horror and a spiking of panic, a cry came from the pram—which turned into a familiar wail as Lola woke from her nap and demanded attention.

CHAPTER THREE

So she *was* upset with how he'd left her. Rico forced his mind from that intriguing nugget of information. He could see that she was torn between wanting to go to her child and wanting him gone, and then she blurted out, over the ever increasing wails, 'Look, now is really not a good time. Please leave us alone.'

Please leave us alone.

Something about those words, the way she said *us*, the hunted look about her face, made Rico dig his heels in. There was some bigger reason she wanted him gone. She felt threatened. That much was crystal-clear.

And, to his utter surprise, the child's piercing wails were not making him want to run in the opposite direction, fast. Gypsy's words, her whole demeanour was intriguing him, and he hadn't found much intriguing at all lately. He wanted answers to her behaviour, wanted to know *why* she wanted him gone so badly, and her crying baby wasn't about to deter him.

That realisation shocked him slightly, as his only experience with kids to date was his four-year-old niece and her baby brother. While they amused him—especially his precocious niece—his younger half-brother's besottedness had left him perplexed. He just didn't really *get* the whole kids thing. And certainly had no intention of having any himself any time soon—not after the childhood he and his brother had endured... But that path led to dark memories he wasn't prepared to contemplate now.

With a brusqueness brought on by those thoughts Rico bit out, 'Shouldn't you see to your child?'

With obvious dismay at his intractability, Gypsy went over to the pram and pulled back the cover. Immediately the child stopped crying, just a few snuffles now as Gypsy cooed at her and leant in to pick her up.

In that moment Gypsy's plea to *please leave us alone* resonated in his head. Rico's skin tightened over his bones imperceptibly. He was aware that he'd tensed and stopped breathing. As if he had some prescience of something about to occur, something momentous. Which was crazy...

* * *

Gypsy lifted out the solidly warm weight of her still sleepy daughter, unable, despite everything, to keep an instinctive smile off her face. Lola was a happy little girl—rarely grouchy, invariably even-tempered and smiley—which was impossible not to respond to. Gypsy might have castigated herself for her behaviour that night, but she'd never for one second regretted Lola, or contemplated not having her.

Gypsy automatically started to take off Lola's outdoor jacket, as she would be warm after her nap, and tried valiantly to ignore the fact that Rico Christofides would now be looking upon his own flesh and blood for the first time. Pushing that scary thought away, she thought surely now he'd balk at the reality of a toddler and leave them alone?

A child demanding attention was hardly conducive to discussing a one-night stand? Surely he'd see that she wasn't in the market for that again? But even at that thought her lower belly clenched with desire, as if in denial.

Lola's coat was off, and she sat up in Gypsy's arms, more awake now. Having spied Rico Christofides she looked at him shyly, leaning into her mother more, sticking her thumb in her mouth—a habit she'd developed as Gypsy had tried to abstain from using pacifiers.

With the utmost reluctance Gypsy followed

her daughter's gaze, knowing what Rico Christofides would be looking at: a delicately built toddler, with wide slate-grey eyes ringed with long dark lashes, slightly darker than pale skin, and a shoulder-length mop of golden corkscrew curls which habitually refused to be tamed. She was adorable. People stopped Gypsy on the street all the time to exclaim over Lola.

At that moment Lola took her thumb out of her mouth and looked at Gypsy, while pointing at Rico Christofides, and said something unintelligible with all the confidence of having uttered a coherent word.

She gave a determined wriggle that Gypsy knew better than to resist, and she had no choice but to put Lola down on her feet and watch as she toddled, still a little unsteady after her nap, over to Rico Christofides, to look up, clearly certain she'd get a warm response. When he just stared down at her, with a slightly shell-shocked expression, Gypsy felt foreboding surround her like a thick ominous fog.

Lola looked from Rico back to Gypsy and then, uncertain because of his lack of response, she came back and held her arms out to Gypsy, who picked her up again and held her close.

'What did you say her name was?' asked Rico after an interminable moment of tense silence, and Gypsy nearly closed her eyes in despair. *He knew.* He'd have to be blind not to know. They had exactly the same uniquely grey eyes, and now that Gypsy had seen him again she could see they shared the same determined chin...and forehead. She was his feminine miniature—a stunning biological example of nature stamping the father's mark on his child so that there could be no doubt she was his.

'Lola,' Gypsy replied faintly.

As if forcing himself to ask the question, not having taken his eyes off Lola yet, he asked hoarsely, 'How old is she?'

Gypsy did close her eyes now—just for a second. The weight of fate and inevitability weighed her down. She was to be given no reprieve, and even if she did try to bluff her way out of this now, and run, she'd have to change her identity to evade Rico Christofides. An impossibility, considering her already precarious circumstances.

'Fifteen months...'

'I didn't hear you,' he said quickly, curtly.

Gypsy winced at the harsh tone of his voice, and said again, with fatality sinking into her bones along with a numbness which had to be shock, 'Fifteen months.'

For the first time his gaze met hers, and she could see what was burning in those increasingly stormy grey depths. Stark suspicion, realisation, shock, horror…all tangled up.

'But,' he said carefully, *too* carefully, 'that's impossible. Because if she's fifteen months old then, unless you slept with someone else directly after me, that would make her…*mine*. And as you haven't contacted me then I can only assume that she *isn't* mine.'

Gypsy's breath became more shallow. She tightened her hold on Lola, who was beginning to pick up on the tension. That sense of guilt surged back; she couldn't deny him this, no matter who he was. She looked directly at Rico Christofides and swallowed. 'I didn't sleep with anyone else. I haven't been with anyone else…since you.' It killed her, but she had to say it. 'And I wasn't with anyone just before…you.' She didn't think it worth mentioning now that she'd only had one previous lover, in college.

Again too carefully, Rico Christofides said slowly, 'So what you're saying is that your daughter is mine? This little girl is my daughter?'

Gypsy nodded jerkily, going hot and cold in an instant. A clammy sweat broke out over her skin, making it prickle. And at that moment, with impeccable timing, clearly bored with the lack of attention, Lola started to squirm and whinge.

Gypsy seized on the distraction. 'She's hungry.

I need to feed her.' And she fled like a coward into the kitchen, where she put Lola into her highchair and started chattering to her saying nonsensical things. She knew she was in shock, close to hysteria—and acutely aware of the man just feet away, who now had the power to rip their lives apart.

Rico wasn't sure if he was still standing. He'd never been so thoroughly shocked, taken by surprise, blindsided in his entire life. All of the control he took for granted had just crumbled around him like a flimsy façade, and he saw how precarious it had really been since he'd taken control of his life at the tender age of sixteen.

He knew anger was there, but couldn't feel it quite yet. He was numbed. And all he could think about was how it had been just those four words which had made him stop: *please leave us alone*. All he could think about was what it had been like to look into that little girl's eyes for the first time and feel as though he'd missed a step, even though he hadn't even been moving.

When she'd toddled over to look up at him with such innocent guile his heart had jolted once, hard, and he'd felt as if he was falling from a great height into an abyss. An abyss of grey eyes exactly the same unique shade as his own, which he'd inherited from his own father. Right now, the most curious sensation flooded him—as if an elusive piece of himself was slotting into place, something he hadn't even been aware was missing from his life.

It was too much. Acting on blind instinct, he crashed out of Gypsy's apartment, through the main door and to his car, where his driver jumped out. Gasping, Rico yanked open the car door and reached inside for what he was looking for. He realised belatedly that it was still raining as he pulled out a bottle of whisky and unscrewed the top, holding it by the neck before taking a deep gulp of the amber liquid.

His driver quickly ducked back into the car, clearly sensing his boss's volatility and his need to be unobserved. With his hand clenched around the bottle, clarity slowly returned to Rico and he welcomed it. This woman had betrayed him in the most heinous way. The worst way possible.

He'd believed that his own biological father had turned his back on him, but in fact he hadn't. His mother and his stepfather had seen to it that he had believed it, though.

And here was Gypsy Butler, repeating history, blithely bringing up his own daughter—his flesh and blood—clearly with no intention of ever letting him know. She'd tried to get him to leave!

He'd vowed at the age of sixteen that he would never be vulnerable or powerless again. That vow had become his life's code when he'd finally found his father and learnt just how terribly they'd both been lied to—for years. Since then, for him trust had become just a word with useless meaning.

The flimsy chance which had led him to choose that restaurant last night made him shudder in horror; at how close he'd come to never knowing of his own daughter's existence. He looked back towards the still open front door and took in the shabby excuse for a house. Resolve solidified in his chest, and he threw the bottle of whisky back into the car.

He knew that his life was about to change for ever, and damned if he wasn't going to change their lives too. There was a deep primal beat within him now not to let Gypsy or his daughter out of his sight again. The fierce and immediate possessiveness he felt, and the need to punish Gypsy for her actions, were raging like a fire within him.

Gypsy was shaking all over, and had to consciously try to calm herself as she finished feeding Lola and listened out for Rico's car taking off. The speed with which he'd left the apartment had in equal measure sent a wave of relief and a wave of anger through her. While it was her worst nightmare to be in this situation, *how* could he reject his daughter so summarily?

She felt a surge of protectiveness for Lola, and cursed Rico Christofides while acknowledging that she'd expected this to be one of his possible reactions. Straight denial and rejection—just as her father had done with her initially.

She told herself that this was a good thing; she'd salved her conscience by telling Rico Christofides, and Gypsy knew that in the long run thcy'd both be better off. At least she could tell her daughter as she grew up who her father was, and that it just hadn't worked out between them. Guilt hit her again when she thought of how her daughter might perceive the disparity in their circumstances, but Gypsy reassured herself that—as she knew well—the fact that Rico Christofides was a multibillionaire did not a father make.

Her own life had been changed for ever when her ill and penniless mother had begged her father to take Gypsy in. He'd been the owner of the company where Mary Butler had been a menial cleaner. An impossibly rich man who had taken advantage of his position and taken her to bed, with all sorts of promises, only to drop her and fire her as soon as she'd told him she was pregnant. Unable to get another job or make rent payments, she'd soon become homeless.

Gypsy had spent her first few months in a women's refuge, where her mother had gone after she'd given birth at Christmas time. Slowly her mother had built up her life again, finding more menial work and eventually getting them both a council flat in a rough part of London.

Gypsy had known from a very young age that her mother wasn't coping, and she'd learnt to watch out for the signs so that she could take care of her. Of them both. Until she'd got home from school one day and found her mother passed out on the couch, with an empty bottle of pills on the floor.

The emergency services had managed to save her—*just*. And the only thing that had stopped them from putting six-year-old Gypsy straight into foster care had been her mother's assurance that she would send her to live with her father. And so Gypsy had eventually gone to live with the father who had never wanted her, and she'd never seen her mother again. She'd only found out later that her father had comprehensively shut her mother out of Gypsy's life.

Forcing her mind away from sad memories, she strained to listen out for the car and still couldn't hear anything. *What was he doing?*

She made sure that Lola had a firm grip of the plastic cup she was drinking from and stood up, heart thumping. The door to the apartment was still open, and she crept over to close it.

With one hand on the door, she heard heavy steps. *He was coming back*. Panic made her clumsy as she tried to shut the door completely, but it was too late. A hand and foot prevented her from closing it, and as she jumped backwards in shock at how quickly he'd moved she heard a laconic drawl, edged with steel.

'You didn't think it would be so easy to get rid of me, did you?'

CHAPTER FOUR

SHE watched, dry-mouthed as Rico Christofides stepped back into the room, closing the door with incongruous softness behind him, angry grey eyes narrowed intently on her, face impossibly grim. Rain clung in iridescent water droplets to his hair and jacket. She had an awful feeling of *déjà-vu*—the same feeling she'd had that day when she'd found her mother unconscious. Everything was about to change and she was powerless to stop it.

The anger she'd felt moments ago at thinking of him rejecting Lola dissipated under a much more potent threat. Just as her father had belatedly and reluctantly swept in and taken over when she'd been six, now Rico Christofides was about to do the same. This was the other reaction she'd expected and feared.

She fought through her fear and bit out through numb lips, 'I don't want you here, Mr Christofides. I never intended you to find out—'

He uttered a curt laugh. '*Clearly* you never intended me to find out. How serendipitous, then, that I just happened to choose *that* restaurant last night, out of the many thousands in London.'

His sensual mouth firmed, and he looked angry enough to throttle Gypsy, but she felt no sense of danger.

'Believe me, it makes my blood run cold to think how close I came to never knowing about this.'

Gypsy heard herself say, as though from a long way away, 'You didn't let me finish. I didn't intend you to find out *like this*. I was going to tell you…at some stage.'

He arched an imperious brow, derision all over his handsome face, 'When? When she turned ten? Or perhaps sixteen? When she was a fully grown person who'd built up a lifetime of resentment for the father who'd abandoned her?' His voice became blistering, his accent thickened. 'Undoubtedly that's what you'd planned, no? Feed her lies and tell her that her father hadn't wanted to know her? Couldn't be bothered to stick around?'

Gypsy shook her head. She was feeling nauseous at the condemnation in his tone. 'No, I…I hadn't planned that at all. I *was* going to tell her—and you—I promise.'

It sounded so flimsy to her ears now. The fact was she'd just proved him right; she'd planned on keeping this from him indefinitely and it made Rico's eyes narrow even more. Gypsy could see the effort it was taking for him not to reach out and shake her. Or perhaps even worse. For the first time she did feel fear, and stepped back.

He noted the move with disgust. 'Don't worry, you and your promises are so far beneath my contempt right now I wouldn't touch you with a bargepole. If you were a man, however...' He didn't need to finish that sentence.

Gypsy bit back the impulse to explain that she'd wanted to use her degree, set up as a prac- tising child psychologist and be solvent before she went looking for him to deliver the news. She'd known how defenceless she would be to someone like him unless she could stand on her own two feet and demonstrate that she was successfully independent. And this situation was proving exactly how right she'd been to be scared.

Yet even now she was impossibly aware of him physically. The way his suit clung to his powerful frame, the way his hands on his hips drew the eye to their leanness. Hips which she could remember running her hands over as he'd thrust into her so deeply that sometimes she still woke from dreams that were disturbingly real...

Half dizzy with shock, and a surge of very unwelcome lust, Gypsy sank down helplessly into the chair behind her. Rico Christofides just looked at her, without an atom of sympathy or concern, even though she could feel her blood draining southwards and knew she must have gone white. She was scared to stand in case she fainted. But she drew on the inner strength which had got her through years of dealing with her domineering father and stood again, albeit shakily.

At that moment a plaintive cry came from the kitchen, and they both turned to see Lola looking from one to the other with huge grey eyes and an ominously quivering lip. Gypsy could see that she was picking up on *her* distress, and moved to take her up and hold her.

With Lola securely on her hip, she looked back to Rico Christofides, slightly shocked to see a stricken look on his face. She steeled herself and said, 'Look, please leave us be. You know now—you know where we are. I don't want anything from you. *We* don't need anything from you.'

He dragged his eyes from Lola to her, and Gypsy felt the cold sting of his condemnation like a whip against her skin. 'Well, I'm afraid that's just not good enough—because I want something from you. *My daughter.* And, until such time as she can speak for herself, *I'll* determine what she needs.'

His effortlessly autocratic tone made chills run up and down Gypsy's spine. It reminded her so much of her father. She instinctively pulled Lola closer. 'I'm her mother. Anything to do with her welfare is *my* decision. I chose to have her on my own. I'm a single mother.'

His eyes speared her then, and she saw a suspicious light. 'You must have deliberately led people to believe that I'd refused to come forward to acknowledge my own daughter. Am I even mentioned on the birth certificate?'

Gypsy blanched and recalled how she'd lied about knowing his identity when asked in the hospital. She'd reassured herself that if she hadn't seen the news that morning she wouldn't necessarily have realised who he was. All of this behaviour; the lying was so unlike her.

She shook her head quickly and visibly flinched when he made a move towards her. For a second she thought he'd rip Lola out of her arms and take her away. Lola started to make sounds of distress.

Rico stopped dead still and said, his face pale with anger, '*Damn* you to hell, Gypsy Butler.

How dare you refuse to name me as her father. You *knew* who I was.'

Gypsy was trying not to shake, and to pacify Lola at the same time, keeping her voice carefully calm. 'I was protecting her, protecting us.'

As if aware of his daughter's distress too, he surprised Gypsy by lowering his voice. But that didn't make it any less angry. 'From *what*? You had no right to take that decision.'

Gypsy couldn't speak. How could she explain to this man that once she'd found out she was pregnant she'd known for sure that he could not be told until she was ready to deal with him?

He was waiting for her response, for her justification. She blurted out, 'I saw you on the news that morning.'

He frowned.

Gypsy went on, 'I saw you come out of court after you'd reduced that woman to a wreck—and all because she tried to prove that her baby was yours.'

Rico slashed a hand through the air and said curtly, 'You know *nothing* of that case. I was making an example of her so that no other woman would be inclined to think they could take advantage of me in such a way.'

Gypsy hitched up her chin. 'So how can you blame me for not running to tell you of *my* pregnancy? You made it clear when you left that morning that you didn't want to see me again, and then I saw how you dealt with a woman who claimed to be the mother of your child.'

Rico bit back the urge to tell Gypsy that he'd regretted his hasty departure; he'd phoned the hotel straight after the court case was concluded, hoping against hope that she mightn't have left. But she had. And he was not about to reveal that weakness now...especially not now.

Gypsy watched as Rico's face became even more implacable and hard. She conveniently left out her myriad other reasons for not telling him. The memory of that woman's humiliation in the face of Rico's cold and very public displeasure was still etched on her brain.

His voice was utterly icy when he spoke. 'The difference in this case is that I *know* we slept together. I'd only ever met that woman socially before, and because I rejected her advances and she had some paltry circumstantial evidence to suggest we might have been intimate she tried to prove that her baby was mine. I insisted on a paternity test and a public court to prove my case.'

Gypsy shivered inwardly. He was as ruthless as her father had said. 'But you ruined that woman's reputation, dragging her through the courts.'

His face was stony. 'She brought it all on herself. She was convinced I wouldn't want to risk the publicity to prove I wasn't the father. I gave her an opportunity to avoid it and she refused, believing I'd be an easy target and pay her off to keep her quiet. Within weeks of the court case she'd admitted who the real father was and was forced to make do with his meagre million euro fortune. Believe me, she does *not* merit your sympathy.'

Gypsy wondered now at the woman's sense of delusion. Anyone could see that Rico Christofides was not a man who would bow to pressure. She tried not to let his explanation sway her, but deep down she had to admit she was surprised. Even so, she asked, 'And yet you believe that Lola might be yours?'

Rico's eyes went to Gypsy's, and something that flared in their depths made her go hot in the face. 'Apart from the fact that you've told me she is, I can be fairly certain that she's mine because the protection I used that night split. When you assured me you'd be safe, I believed you.'

His words fell into the vacuum they'd caused. To Gypsy's horror, all she could remember was that moment when he'd held back from sliding into her to put on protection. Even that had caused her to entreat him desperately, 'Please,

Rico…don't stop now. *Please*.' If anything, she was probably to blame for the protection failing because she'd rushed him. And then she had promised him she'd be safe, fully believing that she had no cause to worry. But she hadn't taken into account how erratic her cycle had grown in the months after her father's death…

He continued, cutting through her shameful memory, 'You dare to ask me this after you ran from me last night, knowing I was the father of your child? You ask me this when looking at her is like looking into a mirror for me?' His mouth twisted. 'But don't worry. I'm not so naïve that I won't get a paternity test done just to make sure. Your insistence that you want nothing from me only leads me to believe that you *do*.' He laughed harshly. 'You can hardly expect me to believe that I managed to impregnate the one woman in the world who wants not a cent of my fortune?'

He didn't allow her to interject.

'Perhaps you intended coming after me when she was old enough and skinny enough from malnutrition that your story would pluck at the heartstrings of the public with maximum effect? Or perhaps you just relish the twisted power of knowing you're denying your own daughter her paternal heritage? You'll do what you can to bleed me dry even while keeping me away from her?'

Gypsy clutched Lola even closer, and in an unconscious move shielded her daughter as much as she could from Rico. She felt fierce as she gave a scathing look around the pathetic flat. 'Do you really think that I would choose to bring up my daughter in *this* just so that I could hatch some cunning extortion plan? Or that I revel in the fact that we're dependent on dodgy storage heating? I am a good mother, and despite our challenging circumstances Lola has wanted for nothing. She is well fed, looked after and loved. She is an extremely happy and secure child.'

Rico looked at Gypsy. Her huge green eyes were luminous, and he realised that the sky had darkened outside. The rain was a torrential downpour now, and he could hear the insistent drip-drip of the leak in the corner and feel the damp in the air.

He could not understand this woman. This whole situation. He was certain he was Lola's father—he *felt* it in his bones in a way he couldn't explain and didn't want to articulate to this woman. So why hadn't she fleeced him from the moment she'd found out she was pregnant? Especially as she'd known who he was. None of this made sense to him.

He asked again, 'Why didn't you tell me?'

Gypsy looked away. He saw her bite her lip. Finally she looked back, and he saw trepidation in her eyes, and something that looked suspiciously like fear. 'Because I wanted to protect my daughter and do what was best for her.'

Rico shook his head, uncomprehending. His brain was quick, faster than most, but right now it felt as if treacle had been poured into it.

'What on earth are you afraid of?'

And Gypsy just said simply, 'This.'

'You're not making sense, woman. How can your present situation be better than what I could have offered?'

At that moment Rico had a vivid insight into how it might have been. The shock of finding out that Gypsy was pregnant, but then coming to terms with it. He would never have had to wonder about her. He would have had her in his bed all this time, to sate himself until he was done with her. A curious sense of loss assailed him.

They could have worked out some mutual arrangement with Lola… But even as he thought that, he knew he wouldn't be happy with a *mutual arrangement*. Things had escalated way beyond that now. Gypsy owed him. He'd missed out on fifteen months of his daughter's life. His daughter looked at him as if he was a stranger because he *was*.

He fought not to be distracted by remembering the illicit thrill which had run through him to hear Gypsy's admission that she hadn't slept with anyone else since him—that he'd been her only one-night stand. She'd been slightly gauche and innocent that night, and she'd been so tight around him—almost like a virgin. At that memory a wave of desire engulfed him.

Gypsy's chin came up and Rico drew on all his control, fought the impulse he had to stride forward and plunder her soft mouth, caress the delicate bones of her jaw.

'There are plenty of people surviving on a lot less than I. Money isn't everything, and I didn't relish the prospect of being hauled through the courts and the tabloids to prove your paternity. It was my decision to have Lola, therefore she's my responsibility.'

Rico fought back the barrage of questions. He sensed that there was a lot more to it than that. But right now he needed to get them out of this godforsaken place. He would have plenty of time to question Gypsy later. She was proving to be an enigma of monumental proportions, but he had no doubt that despite what she said she had an agenda. Every woman did.

CHAPTER FIVE

GYPSY hoped Rico would just take her explanation and leave it at that. She didn't like the look on his face now, though, it was far too determined. And Lola was being far too quiet.

Gypsy turned her head to see that she was just looking at Rico, with big, watchful eyes, thumb in her mouth. Mrs Murphy, Lola's minder, had commented plenty of times that Lola was an 'old soul'.

And then Rico said, 'Get your things together. You're coming with me.'

Gypsy's head whipped around so fast she nearly got whiplash. 'What?'

'You heard me.' Steel ran through his voice. 'I want you to get whatever you need and pack it up. We're leaving this place *now*.'

Gypsy shook her head, panic trickling through her even as the prospect of being whisked away from this flat held undeniable appeal. With anyone but him.

'I'm not going anywhere with you. *We're* not going anywhere.'

Rico folded his arms. 'Why? Because you've got work to go to later?' He clicked his fingers then, as if remembering something. 'Oh, but that's not right, is it? You walked away from your job last night. Not a very responsible thing to do if you're a single parent, is it?'

Gypsy blanched. She'd forgotten for a moment.

And then, as if thinking of something, Rico asked abruptly, 'Who was minding Lola last night?'

Immediately Gypsy was defensive. Her hackles rose—he was already sounding far too proprietorial. 'Mrs Murphy from down the road. She's a retired qualified childminder who looks after Lola in the evenings for some extra cash.'

He bristled. 'You leave *my* daughter with a stranger in this armpit of a street?'

Gypsy bristled right back. 'She's not a stranger, she's a lovely woman, and Lola has always been perfectly safe with her.' Gypsy's conscience struck her then. She knew that if she'd had a choice she wouldn't have been leaving Lola with anyone. 'And,' she added hurriedly, 'Mrs Murphy comes here to mind her, as Lola is usually already down for the night when I go to work.'

'When you *used to* go to work,' Rico amended. He slashed a hand in the air, 'Here or there, it doesn't matter. This street is a minefield of drug abuse and gangs. I won't have you here for one more night.'

Shaking inside, because her worst fears were manifesting themselves, Gypsy said, 'You can't just come in here and turn us upside down like this.'

'Oh?' Rico sneered. 'Because you have such a lovely set-up here and such a perfect routine?' His voice rang with determination. 'This place is not fit for a dog, much less a small child. You are coming with me and you will stay with me tonight.'

Right then Lola reached up to touch Gypsy's face, and she could feel how cold her small hands were. Guilt rushed through her. The storage heating still hadn't come on, and Gypsy knew that even when it did its heat output was not great. Without the supplementary heater things would be bleak, and far colder than usual. It was freezing, it was damp, and she was horribly aware of the leak in the corner—and the fact that Lola had just got over a bad cold.

Rico Christofides couldn't have picked a

worse moment to confront her. *Or a better one,* she realised bitterly.

'What's wrong with her?' Rico asked sharply, his eyes on Lola, who Gypsy could feel getting heavier in her arms.

Weariness struck Gypsy. 'She's tired. She didn't sleep well last night, and she only got a small sleep in the buggy just now.'

Something even more determined crossed Rico's face then. 'I will carry you both out of here bodily if that's what it takes, Gypsy, don't think I won't. We have to talk. You owe me this. And I refuse to stay here a moment longer.'

To her utter shame, Gypsy could feel the fight leaving her. She couldn't in all conscience deny him the chance to talk things over. 'Where are you proposing to take us?'

'To my apartment in town. It's infinitely more comfortable there. I have a housekeeper who can keep an eye on Lola while we talk.'

Feeling as though she was being carried aloft on white water rapids, with the utmost reluctance, Gypsy finally said, 'OK—fine. We'll come with you.'

And then things moved with scary swiftness. Gypsy put a drowsy Lola into her buggy while she got together a bag of essentials. She balked at Rico's assertion that they wouldn't spend another night here, and resolved to make him see he couldn't just waltz in and change their lives, but she packed a small suitcase just in case, knowing well that with a small child she couldn't afford not to be practical.

Finally she was ready, and saw Rico had his coat on again and stood in a wide-legged stance, waiting. He'd asked her about a car seat for Lola, and she'd explained that the buggy seat doubled as one. She'd heard him on his mobile phone, barking out what sounded like orders in Greek. Now he just watched her with cold eyes. So unlike the seductive man who had danced with her in that club that night—not that his effect on her was any less now.

She pushed aside the memory ruthlessly. Her hands were full with bags, and she looked to Lola's pram.

Before she'd articulated anything he moved and said, 'I'll take her. You lock up.'

And before Gypsy could protest or say a word she watched as Rico detached the seat from the buggy frame, as if he'd been doing it all his life, and then lifted the seat up with an ease Gypsy envied. Seeing him cradling the seat with Lola in it made something primal and treacherous rush through her. She wanted to snatch her daughter back from him, and yet her eyes pricked ominously. Gypsy forced the tears aside, knowing that to show any emotion to Rico

Christofides would show him weakness—and she couldn't afford to be weak.

Once the flat door and main door had been closed and locked, Rico let Gypsy go to the car first in the teeming rain, accompanied by the solicitous driver, who held an umbrella over her head. He put her bags in the boot, before helping her into the car. When she was settled, Rico strode forward, Lola protected by his coat. Once at the car, he handed her in to Gypsy, who was all fingers and thumbs securing the seat belt around the chair. Lola was bone-dry and contentedly sucking her thumb—which made Gypsy feel peculiar inside.

As the car slowly pulled away from the kerb she remembered something. 'The buggy!'

Rico all but ignored her, officiously making sure that her own seat belt was fastened. Gypsy wanted to slap his hands away when she felt them brush against her thigh, hating the shiver of heat that went through her lower body. He was far too close, as she'd had to move to the middle of the back seat to accommodate Lola's chair. His musky and uniquely masculine scent wound around her, threatening to make all sorts of memories flood back. It was humiliating in the extreme when he clearly didn't feel the same way, at all.

And who could blame him? Gypsy thought wearily, knowing that she looked not far removed from a homeless person. The only smart clothes she owned were her work clothes, and they were useless now...

He finished and straightened up, and said grimly, 'That pram is the least of your worries. By the time we get to my apartment there will be a new one waiting.'

Gypsy tried not to let the quiet warm luxury of the car seduce her. 'You can't just do this, you know...just because you're her father.'

He turned a blistering grey gaze on Gypsy, and she tried not to quail beneath it. The space in the back of the car was claustrophobic. 'The moment you decided to leave me out of the equation was the moment you started stacking the odds against yourself. I have just as much right to my daughter as you, and now that I know of her existence I will move heaven and earth to ensure that she grows up knowing me.'

He turned away to look out of the window, his profile austere, jaw clenched.

Gypsy closed her mouth firmly. She knew that there was no point in remonstrating further right now. Men like Rico Christofides and her father switched off when they weren't hearing what they wanted or expected to hear.

Gypsy turned her head too, her stomach in

knots, aghast at how easy it was to just stare at him. She looked out of her own window as London slid past in bleak greyness. She just hoped and prayed that when he saw the reality of living with a toddler even for a few hours he'd be all but paying them to go home.

Before long they were in the much more salubrious area of Mayfair. Clean streets, expensive cars, and even more expensive-looking people. It had stopped raining, almost as if they'd left the black cloud behind over Gypsy's dismal street. Distaste curdled her insides; her father had had an apartment here, where he'd housed his various mistresses.

Rico's car drew to a smooth halt outside a sleek building with an awning over the pavement. A doorman rushed to the car to open the door for them. Gypsy got out and extricated Lola, who had fallen asleep during the journey. She stood on the pavement with Lola in her arms, blinking, feeling a little as though she'd been transported to another planet, and half hoping that she might wake up in a minute and see that this had all been a bad dream.

With not a word, and barely a glance, Rico took Gypsy's bags and led the way into the building and into a lift, where he pressed a button that said *P*. She grimaced to herself. *The penthouse*—of course.

When they emerged from the lift into a plush corridor an apartment door stood open, and Gypsy could see an ample-figured middle-aged woman taking delivery of a myriad assortment of boxes, directing the men to somewhere inside the apartment and saying, 'We need it all set up as soon as possible, please.' Then she saw Rico and broke off with a smile. 'Mr Christofides— you're back already! As you can see it's all just arrived. The men won't be two ticks getting it put together, and then I'll make sure it's set up to your satisfaction.'

Rico brought Gypsy from behind him, his hand on her back, making her feel as if she wanted to arch into it. She stood stiffly, Lola heavy in her arms.

'Gypsy, this is Mrs Wakefield—my house-keeper.'

The warmth in his voice made Gypsy suck in a breath. It reminded her too much of how he'd seduced her so easily. She avoided looking at him and smiled tightly at the openly curious woman, who now looked to Lola.

'Ah, what an absolute cherub. Now, you must be tired and famished. I thought she might be sleeping after the car journey, so I've got a little makeshift bed set up in the sitting room if you want to take her through and lie her down.'

More than a little stunned, Gypsy meekly followed the motherly woman through a gleamingly modern reception area to a huge open-plan room decorated in dark greys and muted tones. A bachelor pad if ever there was one.

Mrs Wakefield showed Gypsy where to lie Lola down, and she even had a cashmere blanket to put over her. She confirmed Gypsy's suspicions when she said chattily, 'I have five girls myself, but they're all grown up now. They grow so fast—mark my words, you won't even see the time fly by before she's turning your heart in your chest with boyfriends and wanting to go out all night.'

Gypsy made some trite comment, but she was very aware of Rico, who had followed them in and was standing silently by. She could feel his censorious gaze. No doubt his housekeeper's words were reminding him of how much he'd missed already.

With a promise to return soon, with some tea and sandwiches, she left them alone in the huge room. Gypsy fussed over Lola for a moment, wanting to avoid looking anywhere near Rico.

He asked then, 'Is it normal for her to sleep like this?'

Gypsy finally stood up and crossed her arms.

His question unsettled her, making her defensive. 'She's just catching up. And she normally has a nap in the afternoon anyway.'

Rico's jaw was tight. 'How would I know this?'

Gypsy just looked at him, quashing the dart of guilt, and watched as he took off his coat with jerky movements, before flinging it down over the back of a chair. He started to pace, and Gypsy felt that weariness snake over her again. She hadn't realised how tired she was. But she was exhausted.

In an effort to put some space between them, she moved away and looked around. Floor-to-ceiling windows looked out over London, where clouds made it seem darker, the skyline soaring against them. Despite the grim weather it was enchanting. And completely impractical.

She turned around again, determined, despite the pathetic state of her own flat, not to allow Rico to railroad them. 'We can't stay here for long. This place is a recipe for disaster with a toddler.' She gestured with a hand towards a low glass table. 'There are sharp edges and corners everywhere. Lola's far too inquisitive at the moment—she'll get hurt.'

Rico stood with hands in his pockets, grey eyes narrowed on Gypsy, who could feel a flush rising over her chest and her face. All of a sudden she felt hot, and wanted to take off some layers.

'I will make sure Lola is protected. Within twenty-four hours this apartment will be child-proofed. You'll have to come up with more than such a flimsy pretext to deter me, Gypsy.'

Suspicion and a trickling of cold horror gripped her then, and she asked, 'Those men… what were they delivering?'

Rico ticked off on his fingers. 'A pram, a cot, a changing table… I told my assistant to make sure all the basics were bought and delivered. You can let me know what's missing.'

Gypsy's hands dropped to her sides. 'But…I just came to talk…for one evening…one night. We are going home tomorrow. I have work to find, and Lola's in a routine.' Hysteria was rising. 'You have no right to presume anything. We don't need all that for one night, so you're just going to have to get it taken away again.'

Rico advanced on Gypsy, and she fought not to snatch up Lola, turn and run. He came and stood before her with a look of almost *savage* intent on his face, in his eyes, and Gypsy knew that this was the moment she'd realised just how formidable he was going to be.

'That child is my daughter. I have missed fifteen months of her existence—fifteen months of her development and watching her grow. As far as she's aware she has no father. It doesn't matter that she might be too young to realise the import of that now, *I* do. Know this, Gypsy Butler: as of this day, and from now on, I am in her life and your life. And you, with no job and living in a hovel, are in no position to argue with my wishes.'

Conversely, even as his words horrified Gypsy, she felt on more even ground. She knew what she was dealing with now. She asked, 'Are you threatening me, Rico? Are you saying that if I were to leave with Lola right now, walk out of here, you would bring down the full force of your power on us?'

A muscle jumped in his jaw. His eyes were so dark they looked almost black and not grey. Eventually he said with chilling calm, 'That's exactly what I'm saying. If you were to walk out of here right now, the only way I would allow it to happen was if you were to leave *alone*.' He smiled, and it was feral, 'But, based on the evidence of how determined you've been to keep her from me and all to yourself, I don't think you'll be doing that.'

The implication that he would quite happily let *her* walk away sent something dark to Gypsy's gut. 'You're right. I wouldn't dream of leaving my daughter behind. As for our situation—yes, we're vulnerable, and certainly in no position to fight you should you decide that it's necessary. So of course I'm not stupid enough to encourage your wrath. I know how men like you operate, Rico Christofides. You have no compunction about squashing the opposition just so long as you get whatever it is that takes your fancy at the time. We'll bow to your wishes for now, as we have little choice, but I don't doubt that as soon as you've seen the reality of setting up home with a small child you'll be throwing us back to where we came from, so you can get on with your self-absorbed existence and your bid for world domination. And as far as I'm concerned that moment can't come soon enough.'

Gypsy stopped talking. She was breathing hard. Rico was just looking at her, far too assessingly, and she cursed herself for having said too much. But, as she knew well from experience, it *would* be utterly futile to fight with someone like him. Better to indulge him, let him play out his father role, and wait for him to get bored. She had no doubt he would—especially with red-haired beauties like the one last night waiting in the wings. At the thought of him sleeping with her something even darker clenched in Gypsy's gut.

Just then Mrs Wakefield bustled back into the room, with tea and sandwiches, and Lola woke up, struggling out of her makeshift bed.

Gypsy rushed to help her off the couch, and automatically lifted her away from the hazardous glass coffee table. Lola slipped out of her hands again, like a wriggling eel, and toddled over to the huge window, fascinated by the staggering view.

She pointed when a bird flew past and exclaimed, 'Birdy!'

Mrs Wakefield finished putting out the tea and went over to make friends with a clearly delighted Lola. After a few minutes of largely nonsensical but earnest chatter from the toddler, she turned to Gypsy, 'She's a sunny one, isn't she?'

Gypsy smiled wryly, glad of the momentary distraction. 'Most of the time, yes. But woe betide anyone who gets close when she's tired or hungry...'

Mrs Wakefield held out a hand, and Lola took it trustingly. 'Why don't we go off for a little exploring and let Mum and Mr Christofides have their tea?'

Before Gypsy could protest Lola was happily toddling out of the room with Mrs Wakefield, not a care in the world at leaving her mother behind. And while Gypsy felt proud, because it was a sign of a happy and secure child, she also felt absurdly hurt.

When she turned around Rico was holding

out a chair at the larger table for her to sit down, and he said mockingly, 'Don't worry. She's not going to kidnap her or spirit her away.'

Gypsy said nothing, just sat down, still a little shocked at what had spilled out of her mouth only moments before. Clearly she was feeling far too volatile at the moment to be sure of remaining calm and rational. With grim reluctance she finally slipped off her coat, knowing they wouldn't be returning to her flat any time soon.

Rico poured tea and pushed some sandwiches towards Gypsy. She was avoiding his eyes again, and he was still reeling slightly at her outburst. The fact that she was projecting something deeply embedded within her onto him was obvious. He suspected it was the same thing that had stopped her from automatically telling him about her pregnancy. But what?

His interest piqued, he vowed, among everything else he'd already set in motion, to look into Gypsy Butler's life for clues. The fact that he knew nothing about the mother of his child did not sit well with him. If he had ever contemplated having a child with anyone, he knew he was the kind of person to have chosen someone based on cool logic and intellect. The mother of his child would not be left to fate and circumstance, the child would not be conceived in a moment of blind passion— His stomach clenched. But that was exactly what had happened…

But, he reassured himself, he had the means to control that. To control *her*. He watched her eat the sandwiches with relish, and wondered how long it had been since she'd eaten properly. Her baggy shapeless clothes hung off her petite frame, and that slightly plump litheness he remembered so well was gone. Even so, he conceded reluctantly, it did nothing to diminish her appeal or douse his desire.

Abruptly he stood, cup in hand, and went to look out of the window. He didn't like the way she could rouse him so effortlessly, or the way he cared even for a moment that she'd grown thin. And especially he didn't like the way he felt inclined to do everything in his power to restore that vivacious health.

He turned to face her and she was looking at him with big wary eyes. Very like the way Lola had been looking at him in the flat. Her hand was clenched around her cup, a tiny crumb at the corner of her mouth. Her wildly curling hair lay around her shoulders, reminding him of that free spirit image she'd projected when he'd first seen her, which had pulled him to her like a magnet. It made him think for an uncomfortable moment that perhaps she *was* someone who wouldn't be influenced by his wealth.

He steeled himself and reminded himself of exactly what she'd done to him. *The worst thing possible.* Distaste and disgust for the type of woman she was, for the type of mother she was, rose up within him and he welcomed it. On the evidence of her reluctance to inform him about Lola she might not be a gold-digger, but she was something worse. She was the kind of woman who wouldn't hesitate to marry another man and have him bring her daughter up as if she were his own, uncaring of the cataclysmic fall-out that would ensue.

He reacted to the way she was still looking at him, with trepidation mixed with a kind of defiance. 'You *do* know that I'll never forgive you for this, don't you?'

CHAPTER SIX

'YOU *do know I'll never forgive you for this,
don't you?'*

The words resounded in Gypsy's head as
she lay wide awake in the softest bed imagin-
able much later that night. It had taken ages
to put Lola down after she'd been fed, bathed
and changed. The penthouse was far too exciting for her—plus the attention of not only Rico
but a clearly besotted Mrs Wakefield, who had
been the soul of discretion even though Gypsy
had seen her looking assessingly from Lola to
Rico.

To see Lola running around the cavernous
rooms had made Gypsy's chest ache, very aware
of how cramped their own space was…

Mrs Wakefield had shown Gypsy around the
entire apartment, and brought her to an enor-
mous suite where a cot had been set up by the
king-sized bed. An impromptu nursery had been
made in the dressing room. A huge bathroom

completed the suite, and Gypsy had seen from a brief look into Rico's own rooms, stamped with his masculine touch, that he had an even larger suite.

The housekeeper had told her how to get around the kitchen, and shown her where everything was. Gypsy had been bemused more than shocked to see the fridge and cupboards were already stocked high with an assortment of baby food, and the formula she'd requested. There had even been baby monitors, so that Gypsy could keep one with her as she moved about the apartment in case she didn't hear Lola wake.

Lola slept nearby now, and Gypsy could hear her baby breaths, light and even. Usually the sound comforted her, but her stomach hadn't unclenched all evening—or, in truth, since she'd seen Rico just last night. *Just last night.* It was hard to believe that within the space of twenty-four hours she was ensconced in his apartment. But then, she surmised grimly, she'd feared exactly this kind of autocratic takeover all along.

And yet her conscience niggled her. While he was being just as controlling as her father had been, she couldn't deny the fact that, unlike her father, Rico was showing nothing but signs of accepting Lola.

He'd come into the kitchen where she'd been making herself some cocoa after putting Lola down for the night and said coolly, 'I've arranged for my doctor to come in the morning. He'll take swabs from Lola and I, and we'll have paternity proved within the week.'

Without giving her a chance to say a thing, he'd continued relentlessly, 'I don't see any point in your going anywhere until we have the results of the paternity test, so you will remain here for the week. Once it's established that I'm Lola's father, the first thing we will see to is amending the birth certificate so that my name is added.'

Utterly remote and cold, he'd inclined his head then, and said, 'If you'll excuse me? I have some work to attend to in my study. I trust you know your way around now?'

Gypsy had nodded, intimidated by this ice-cold man. 'Mrs Wakefield was more than helpful.'

'Good.' And without another word he'd strode out of the kitchen.

Gypsy had heard a sound then, on the baby monitor. Straining her ears, she'd just been able to make out that Rico must have gone in to look down on Lola. Her heart had lurched treacherously at realising that. There was silence for a long moment. She'd heard his breath, and then something indistinct that sounded like Spanish.

With a shiver, Gypsy realised that even if his initial acceptance of his own flesh and blood wasn't mirroring her father's cold rejection of *her* the outcome would be the same. Rico was staking his claim, vowing not to let his daughter be taken away from him. Vowing to make Gypsy pay...just as her father had done to her mother—albeit for different reasons.

In Gypsy's case, once Social Services had been involved, and her father had had no choice but to acknowledge her, he'd made sure that Gypsy had never seen her mother again. It had only been in later years that she'd discovered that her mother had died alone in a mental hospital just a few years after that awful day.

Gypsy had always suspected that nothing much had been wrong with her mother other than a tendency to depression, which could have been exacerbated by her birth and their tough circumstances. She'd been a mournful woman, prone to pessimism, and not very strong. But nothing that a little support mightn't have helped.

Her father had cut Mary out of Gypsy's life ruthlessly, and even though he'd had information as to her whereabouts he'd refused to help her at all. He'd let her be sucked into the labyrinthine mental health-care system, eventually to die. After her father's death Gypsy had found heart-breaking letters from her mother, begging for his help, begging for a chance to see Gypsy again. It had been almost too much to bear...

Gypsy sighed deeply and tried her best not to think of that now. Tried not to think of how it had killed her inside to realise the night she'd met Rico that she had found it so easy to gravitate towards a man of her father's ilk. Was there something within her that resonated with powerful and ruthless men, despite what her father had done to her and her mother?

She sighed again, and turned over to face where Lola slept so peacefully. Her father was gone. And, while she might be in this untenable situation with Rico now, she was *not* like her mother. She would not be so easily separated from her daughter. She was infinitely stronger and more resourceful. They would get through this, and she would *not* let him consume them utterly just because he craved control.

The following morning, early, Rico sat at the breakfast bar in the state-of-the-art kitchen. The *Financial Times* couldn't hold his interest. He looked around and grimaced, seeing for the first time exactly what Gypsy had seen yesterday evening. The place *was* a potential minefield for an innocent toddler. Watching how Lola had gleefully run around last night, having to be plucked from danger every two seconds, had made him sweat. He'd never had to account for a small child before.

His heart clenched at recalling her vibrant energy, and how right it had felt to have her here—how quickly he'd felt that if anyone so much as looked at her the wrong way he'd want to flatten them.

She was beautiful—more beautiful than anything he could have imagined. She was bright, sharp, inquisitive. And, he had to concede grudgingly, all the evidence pointed to the fact that Gypsy was indeed a good mother.

Finding Gypsy in the kitchen making hot chocolate last night had made him feel unaccountably off-centre. Because she'd looked *right* in that domestic milieu. It had been almost as if he couldn't remember a time when this penthouse had just been his London *pied-à-terre*, a place where he invited his mistresses for transitory pleasures. The sense of triumph had disturbed him, making him sound more caustic than he'd intended when he'd outlined his plans for the week.

When he'd gone to look in on Lola as she'd slept, a wave of emotion he'd never felt before had nearly felled him. His hand had shaken as he'd reached out to stroke soft skin—soft as a rose petal. And he had known in that moment, as he'd looked down at her flushed and downy cheeks, at the riot of golden curls around her head and that tiny, fragile and yet so sturdy body, that he was possibly falling in love for the first time.

As for her mother... Rico welcomed the hardness that settled in his chest at just thinking of her. All he felt for Gypsy was a singular irritating desire, which he hated to acknowledge, and the need to seek vengeance. To make her bend to his will. To punish her for keeping their daughter secret from him.

Just then he heard Lola's cry come from the baby monitor, which Gypsy had obviously left in the kitchen last night. She cried out again, and the cries became more forceful as she woke up. Rico tensed all over. Silently he cursed Gypsy. Why wasn't she attending to their daughter? Perhaps something was wrong?

Feeling a very unwelcome sense of panic, Rico was about to stride from the room when he heard Gypsy's soft, sleep-filled and husky voice. 'Good morning, sweetheart...'

He heard the rustle of movement but still couldn't relax; hearing Gypsy's voice was sending a new kind of tension through his body.

'Did you sleep well, my love?'

Lola cooed in response, and Rico heard the sound of kisses. Heat flooded his body.

'I bet you did…you're my best girl, aren't you?'

With an abrupt move, Rico shut off the monitor. The problem was she was *his* girl now too, and the sooner Gypsy came to terms with that the better.

He finished his coffee with one gulp and went to his study to make some calls.

Gypsy was just finishing feeding Lola her breakfast when Rico walked into the kitchen. Immediately her heart thumped hard, and she felt self-conscious in the same baggy jeans and an ancient college T-shirt, with her hair dragged up and held in place with a big clip.

Lola grinned happily at Rico, sending specks of food flying as she waved her spoon around and chattered in baby-speak. Immediately aware of how pristine Rico was in comparison to her, in his dark trousers and white shirt, Gypsy leapt up to get a cloth and wipe the floor.

His voice came curtly. 'Leave it. Mrs Wakefield will see to it.'

She flushed, but sat back down again. 'I don't want to give her any more work to do.'

Rico smiled tightly. 'While your concern is

commendable, Mrs Wakefield has a veritable army of cleaners under her, so don't worry about it.'

He leaned back against the fridge and looked with such indulgence at Lola that Gypsy found it hard to breathe. Then his expression changed visibly to something much cooler as he looked at her. 'I trust you slept well?'

She nodded, watching as Lola grabbed her cup. She was getting to that age when she was determined to do everything herself. 'Yes. Very well. I'm lucky that Lola has always been a pretty good sleeper, and she was tired last night.'

'*You* look tired,' he said abruptly, and when Gypsy glanced up she could see his face flush, as if he was angry with himself for noticing.

She shrugged, feeling even more self-conscious and haggard. 'I've been working hard...' She amended it, '*Was* working hard.'

He obviously noticed her T-shirt and asked now, 'You went to London University?'

Gypsy busied herself cleaning Lola, who squirmed to get away. She hated having to tell him anything, but nodded and said, 'I studied psychology, and specialised in child psychology.'

'When did you graduate?'

'Two years ago.' Just weeks before she'd met

Rico in that club. Not that she was going to mention *that* now.

Rico finally walked over to the coffee machine, and with his intense regard off her for a moment Gypsy could breathe again. She cast his broad back a quick glance. 'I'll need to go out today to get some things for Lola. I need nappies and some other supplies.'

Rico turned around and leaned back easily against the counter, coffee cup in hand. 'I've taken the day off work. My doctor will be here in about an hour to take the swabs and then we can go out together. We can get what you need, and there's a park near here where Lola can play for a bit. We'll have to stay out of the apartment anyway, as people are coming in to child-proof it.'

Surprise washed through Gypsy at the speed with which Rico was adapting his world to accommodate Lola—and also, she had to admit, the fact that he wasn't already gone to work, having left behind an impersonal note, or indeed no note. On the contrary, he was taking a day off. She couldn't remember one instance when her own father, or her vacuous stepmother, had taken a day off for her. Not even on school sports days. Not even on the day when she'd come to her father's home to move in. His cold housekeeper had brought her to a room and told her to stay there until dinnertime.

Feeling unaccountably threatened, and vulnerable from the memory, Gypsy said churlishly, 'Afraid that if you turn your back we'll be gone?'

Rico's eyes flashed, but he took a lazy sip of coffee and drawled, 'Let's just say that trust is certainly an issue.'

She couldn't say anything in response. She didn't want to let him know how much he was surprising her. 'We'll be ready after I've washed and changed Lola.'

Rico put down his coffee cup then, and for a second Gypsy could have sworn that something intensely vulnerable flashed across his face. But it was gone before she could be sure.

'Good,' he said curtly, and watched as Gypsy's jaw tightened in response.

She lifted Lola up to take her out of her seat. Rico had to school his features. For a second an impulse had risen up out of nowhere to offer to help with Lola. It had come out of a desire to get to know her better, to know her routine, watch what Gypsy did with her. Rico forced himself to remember that if he hadn't seen Gypsy in the restaurant he'd still be unaware of the fact that he was a father.

* * *

Gypsy walked into the bedroom later that day, exhausted, and succumbed for a moment to sit on the bed. She felt upside down and inside out. After the genial and twinkly-eyed doctor had been and gone that morning, having taken swabs from Lola and Rico, Rico had changed into jeans and a thick jumper and they'd gone out, wrapped up against the cold. Clearly he didn't trust them to be further than ten feet away from him.

They'd gone to the local shops, where Gypsy had bought what she needed, insisting on paying, much to Rico's obvious chagrin. He'd looked ridiculously out of place in the local pharmacy. And then they'd gone to a local park, where Rico had largely ignored her and focused on Lola, who had basked happily in this new friend's attention. Now, after holding herself so tightly for hours, and being so excruciatingly aware of Rico's physicality, Gypsy's defences were extremely shaky.

Rico's unquestioning certainty that Lola was his still stunned Gypsy. And the fact that Lola was out in the living room right now, playing happily with Rico, made Gypsy feel very funny.

Gathering her energy again, she went to the nursery to get a bib for Lola's dinnertime. When she opened the door she gasped out loud, belatedly remembering Rico's scathing looks at her flimsy nondescript clothes that morning. She'd heard him making sporadic calls on his phone during the day but hadn't thought much of it till now...

In shock, she took in what had to be thousands of pounds worth of clothes for her and Lola, hanging up or put away in drawers. The temporary nursery had been moved to a little ante-room off the bathroom, and was kitted out with even more accessories.

A potent memory of her father made her vision blur with anger. At the age of thirteen she'd been mesmerised when she'd seen the profusion of beautiful clothes he'd bought for her—until she'd realised to her shame and horror that they were all either too big or too small. And that he'd bought them specifically for her to wear socially, at his side, not out of any genuine paternal affection. He'd forced her to wear them, reading her acute embarrassment as ungrateful thanks. He'd had no comprehension of a daughter on the threshold of puberty, with a rapidly developing body.

And now Rico had taken a decision to do more or less the same thing. At no point during the day had he even asked her opinion. Or suggested that they go shopping together. Not that she would have complied, she knew grimly, but it would have been nice to be consulted. He was *buying* them—throwing money at the problem.

Gypsy gathered up some of the baby clothes, with their ostentatious designer labels, and stalked into the living room, where Rico was standing at the window with Lola held high, pointing things out. He looked around, those grey eyes glowing, only to rapidly cool as he took in Gypsy's stiff stance.

'What's the meaning of this?' She held the clothes out stiffly, some falling to the ground.

Rico's eyes flashed as he turned to face her. 'You're both in dire need of new wardrobes. I can provide that.'

'I've already told you,' Gypsy spat, 'we don't need you, or your money. To spend money on clothes this expensive is pure extravagance. There's enough in there to clothe an entire village of babies, not just one. As it is, Lola's growing so fast that she'll have outgrown most of them before she can even wear them.'

Rico's face tightened, a muscle moving in his jaw, and Gypsy felt like a complete bitch. Because she had the strangest sensation that she'd just hurt him.

'I will provide for my daughter. That is non-negotiable. And while you are with me, under

my roof, you will *not* go outside the door looking like a bag lady.'

'God forbid,' Gypsy muttered caustically,
somehow relieved that Rico was retaliat-
ing, 'that we should embarrass the great Rico
Christofides.' She put down the rest of the
clothes and held her hands out for Lola, who
squirmed to get to Gypsy. 'It's time for her
dinner now.'

After an interminable moment full of crackling tension Rico finally handed her over, and
bit out, 'I'll be in my study for the rest of the
evening. If you're so concerned about the excess
of clothes, take out what you think she won't
need and I'll have them sent back.'

And then he walked out, and Gypsy inexplicably felt like a complete heel.

A couple of hours later she sat by Lola's cot,
watching her fight against sleep, her eyes getting heavier and heavier. And Gypsy was still
fighting that feeling of guilt. Because Rico was
all at once confirming every one of her worst
suspicions and yet confounding them at the
same time. The image of Lola in his arms earlier was still clear, and she knew she'd been a
coward in not acknowledging how it had made
her feel—knew too that her knee-jerk reaction
to the clothes had come from somewhere that

had much more to do with painful memory than the present situation.

In his study at the same moment, Rico looked impossibly grim as he picked up his phone. When someone answered, he bit out tersely, 'Gypsy Butler. I want you to find out everything you can about her. Money is no object.'

When he put the phone down Rico took another gulp of whisky from the bulbous glass and passed a weary hand over his face. Women caused not a ripple in his life: they were there, they were willing, and he always chose the most beautiful and experienced. *Until that night*, when everything he'd thought he knew had blown up in his face...

No woman, *ever*, had made him want to simultaneously throttle her and kiss her. His mouth curled up in a feral smile. Kissing Gypsy certainly would help assuage the near-constant ache in his groin, but he could well imagine the resistance she would undoubtedly put up. She tensed whenever he came near her, but he could see the signs of attraction. It hummed between them like a current of electricity.

Domination of this woman was rapidly becoming his life's obsession, and sensual domination over her rebellious nature was going to be sweet indeed. For the first time since he could

remember work was taking a back seat in his
life. Going shopping was something he hadn't
indulged in in a long time. It had reminded
him uncomfortably of the night when he'd met
Gypsy in the club, and he had ducked into an
all-night pharmacy to get protection, like an out-
of-control teenager.

He'd felt uncomfortably exposed when she'd
pointed out his impulsive gesture to spoil his
daughter. How could he explain to Gypsy that
he wanted the chance to lavish everything on
Lola that he'd been denied up till now? He'd felt
exposed and weak; no one had made him feel like
that in a long time and he didn't welcome it.

Perhaps when he'd had Gypsy again he would
be able to see clearly how best to slot her into
his life. She had to want *something*, despite her
apparent moralistic outrage at his wealth; she'd
made a big song and dance earlier, insisting on
paying for everything—Rico couldn't remember
the last time a woman had insisted on paying for
anything—but once he knew what it was Gypsy
wanted, what her weakness was, he would manipulate her to his ends. The most important
thing for now was to ensure that he bound both
Gypsy and Lola to him as tightly as he could.
They weren't going anywhere for the foreseeable
future.

* * *

The following evening Gypsy fumed and seethed. She paced along the huge window in the living room and glared at the view. The apartment was quiet. Mrs Wakefield had gone home and Lola was asleep.

When they'd woken that morning Gypsy had found a note from Rico.

I'll be at the office all day. Call me if you need anything.

He'd listed a number. Gypsy had breathed a sigh of relief, but had momentarily felt an uncomfortable spiking of something suspiciously like disappointment.

It had been later, when she'd been in the hallway, putting the last of the bags full of new clothes she'd decided she and Lola didn't need—which was most of them—that she'd noticed the tabloid newspapers.

Mrs Wakefield had confided to her that they were her weakness, and that Rico got them delivered each day for her. Something had caught her eye, and she'd opened the top one out to see a grainy picture of Rico, herself and Lola in the park the day before.

Rico had Lola in his arms, and Gypsy stood to one side smiling. She couldn't even remember that she had been smiling, and it felt like a treachery to see it now. The headline screamed out: *Tycoon Rico's secret family!*

In horror, Gypsy had thrown the paper down. With anger boiling upwards she'd tried to call him, but hadn't been able to get past the clipped secretary who'd said officiously, 'I'm terribly sorry but Mr Christofides can*not* be disturbed at the moment if it's not urgent. I'll pass on a message?'

Gypsy had bitten out, 'Tell Mr Christofides that his *secret family* would like to talk to him.'

He'd planned it—she knew he must have planned it. To make sure that it was out there in the public domain that he had a child. So that they wouldn't be able to make a move without being followed.

Sure enough, when Gypsy had rung down to the doorman he'd sounded bewildered and confirmed that, yes, there suddenly seemed to be hundreds of photographers outside the door. To think that she had been *surprised* by Rico's apparent willingness to spend time with them.

The apartment door opened at that moment and Gypsy turned round, hands clenched into fists at her sides. With her heart thumping she waited, and watched as Rico's powerful frame appeared in the doorway. He was tugging at his tie and looked tired. She quashed the concern.

'Thank you for calling me back today.' Sarcasm dripped from her voice.

His eyes burned a dark grey, no expression on his face. 'I got the message.'

Gypsy was starting to shake at his non-response. 'Do you know that if I hadn't seen the tabloids and had gone out with Lola we would have been ambushed by the hundreds of photographers outside? As it was we couldn't leave all day, and to keep a toddler cooped up in an apartment—even one as large as this—is not a pleasurable experience.'

He walked further into the room and pulled off his tie, flicking it down onto a sofa while his large hand went to open the top button of his shirt. Gypsy wanted to back away, but couldn't as the window was already at her back.

'I heard about the tabloids getting pictures. There were bodyguards waiting outside. You would have been protected.'

Gypsy threw up her hands. 'Oh, I'm sorry—is that something I'm just meant to know by osmosis? And what good would bodyguards have been with a hundred paparazzi snapping pictures of me and my child?'

He came closer, and Gypsy could see the glorious olive tone of his skin, that stunning bone structure, and the slightly crooked nose which hinted at a past which contained violence.

Despite his urbane exterior, a sense of barely leashed danger oozed out of him.

His mouth was grim. 'I didn't call you back because I was involved in intricate negotiations and could *not* break away.'

Gypsy smiled bitterly. 'Oh, I'm sure you were. Nothing is as important as *negotiations*, or making your next million.'

His eyes flashed at that, but he just said, 'I knew you and Lola were safe. If I'd thought for a second you were calling about something serious—'

Gypsy gasped. 'That *was* serious! Our safety was compromised, and we were forced to stay inside like fugitives. Not to mention the fact that our faces are all over the tabloids and everyone is wondering who this *secret family* is.'

Horror trickled through Gypsy at the thought of people digging and finding out about her history. She had a very real fear that if Rico found out who her father had been, and what she had done when he'd died, he would hold it against her—use the information to make her seem like a weak mother. And if he ever found out about her mother's mental instability...

Fear galvanised her as she squared up to Rico. 'I'm leaving in the morning. Taking Lola with me, back to our flat. Your plans are not going to work. I have rights as Lola's mother. I've given you a chance to see her, but I will not let our lives be turned upside down like this.'

Gypsy went to stalk past Rico, but he caught her arm in a bruising grip.

She looked up and tried not to be aware of how tall he was. 'Let me *go*.'

His mouth was a grim line. 'You're not going anywhere, Gypsy. We don't have the test results back yet, and that mob outside will follow you and hound you until they know every last detail of your life.'

He articulated her fears exactly. Bitterness blinded her. 'Which is exactly what you planned, isn't it? You expect me to believe that you didn't *know* about the pictures? Tell me—is one of those filthy editors your friend? Can you feed him stories when you want? Manipulate things to suit you? Manipulate *us*?'

It had been one of her father's favoured *modus operandi*—the manipulation of the media.

'*No.*' Rico sounded incensed, insulted. A muscle clenched in his jaw. 'Of course not. The paparazzi are always on my trail. I'll admit I was aware of them lurking yesterday—and, yes, I'll admit that the thought of some pictures turning up didn't bother me too much. But I didn't anticipate this level of interest.'

His hand was still on her arm, making Gypsy feel all sorts of sensations, making her forget why she was so angry. He was so close—too close. She tried to pull away but his hold increased. She felt desperation rise.

'Let me go, Rico. You had no right to expose us like that, and you didn't mind the thought of pictures turning up because you had to realise that it would constrain our movements. No wonder you went back to work today. I'm taking Lola tomorrow, and we'll leave London if we have to.'

Rico whirled her so fast that Gypsy lost her balance and only stayed standing because he gripped both her arms. He stared down at her and she was mesmerised by his eyes. He shook his head, and his harsh hold on her arms inexplicably gentled, even though he was silently telling her of his refusal to let her go. His eyes roved her face, and Gypsy's mouth tingled betrayingly where his eyes rested on it for a long moment.

To her utter chagrin and horror she couldn't remember exactly why she and Lola had to get away so badly. She was back in time, staring up at Rico for the first time and thinking that he had to be looking at someone else—he couldn't be looking at *her* like that.

His hands drew her closer, and Gypsy felt her feet moving against some dim and distant will she was trying to impose.

Rico was finding it hard to remember what they'd been talking about. He was forgetting the tinge of guilt he'd felt at Gypsy's accusation. While he certainly hadn't intended for them to be hounded by the press, he *had* seen the advantage in allowing it to become public knowledge that he had a daughter. But now, as he looked down into Gypsy's deep green eyes, all that faded.

His voice was rough and deep. The words felt as if they were being pulled out of him. 'Dammit, I still want you. I couldn't forget about you, no matter how hard I tried. That's why I came after you.'

Gypsy fought the clamour of her pulse, threatening to suck her under. Everything she'd been angry about was disappearing under a wave of need so strong it was making her shake. She fought not to give in to Rico's pull, and said scathingly, 'You were thinking of me even as you slept with that woman the other night?'

He smiled, and it was pure danger, 'Jealous, Gypsy? Because if you are then surely that means you haven't been able to forget about me either.'

'Damn you to hell, Rico,' Gypsy said shakily. Too many nights when she'd woken aching for this man's touch were mocking her now.

'Well, if I'm going to hell then you're coming with me.'

He pulled her right into him, and her T-shirt and jeans were no barrier against his long, lean, *hardening* body. A tremor of pure arousal shot through her as his head descended. For a split second Gypsy tried to articulate something negative, but their breaths were mingling, and then his mouth was slanting over hers with expert precision and she was lost…

She was back in time, on the street outside that club, after putting her hand over Rico's mouth because she didn't want to know his name, because she didn't want any kind of reality to intrude on the moment. And he'd pulled her into him and kissed her for the first time.

The kiss then, as now, had been the culmination of an intense build-up. His mouth was hard and firm, and yet soft enough to make her melt and yearn and lean into him even more. Tacitly telling him of her approval, of her desire. Rico groaned deep in his throat and deepened the kiss, plundering Gypsy's mouth, finding her tongue and stroking along it with erotic mastery. His hands had moved down to clasp her hips, fingers digging into her waist. Her hands clung to broad shoulders. She could feel her hair loosen from its topknot and fall down over her shoulders.

Between her legs she was burning up, the ache she'd been feeling for two years growing more acute with each passing second, with the tantalising promise of fulfilment. As if reading her mind, Rico pulled her even closer, his big hands spreading around her buttocks to lift her against him slightly, so that she could feel his arousal more fully.

And all the while their mouths clung, and a desperation was building in the kiss, as if they'd both suddenly realised the depth of the passion they'd been missing for two years. Gypsy strained higher, her hands going to Rico's head, where her fingers tangled in silky strands, keeping his head against hers. Not allowing him to escape...

With another guttural moan, Rico impatiently found and pushed up Gypsy's T-shirt, smoothed his hand up over her waist and belly to cup her breast. With a gasp she couldn't hold back she tore her mouth away from Rico's and looked up—dazed, dizzy.

At that moment a little squeak came from the baby monitor. They both tensed and froze. The red mist of arousal cleared from Gypsy's brain and the present moment came back. She was plastered to Rico's front, all over him like a clinging vine. And his hand cupped her lace-covered breast intimately.

No other sound came from the monitor, but Gypsy used the impetus to push roughly away from Rico, who stood there looking dishevelled and utterly gorgeous, cheeks flushed, eyes so dark they looked black in the dim lighting. More buttons on his shirt had been opened. Horror gripped her. Had she done that?

She backed away and hit the window, was glad of the support. She felt as though she might just slide down it and land in a heap of sprawled limbs. 'I don't know...' she began shakily '...that was...'

'That,' Rico said grimly, sounding utterly composed, 'was something we will return to—without interruption.'

Gypsy shook her head, and quivered as Rico strode forward and caged her in, putting his hands either side of her head on the thick glass.

'We've just proved that this desire has not died. If I were to seduce you right here and now I could have your legs around my waist and take you right against this window.'

The carnality of his words made Gypsy blush brick-red, even as the image in her mind strangled any denial she might make. She just shook her head again—pathetically.

Rico brought a finger to her cheek and trailed it slowly and sensuously down over her jaw, and lower, to the V of her T-shirt which rested just above her cleavage. His eyes met hers. 'You won't be going anywhere, Gypsy. Not until I say so.' A chill entered his voice. 'And if you do, I'll find you. So you see, no matter where you go, I'll simply bring you back. You and Lola are mine now, and I always claim what's mine.'

At that moment the monitor sprang to life again, and Gypsy jumped. A plaintive wail sounded. *'Mama...'*

'I hate you, Rico.'

He smiled, and it didn't reach his eyes. 'I hate you too, Gypsy. But conveniently enough our desire seems to exist in spite of our mutual antipathy.'

Gypsy finally managed to bring her hands up to knock Rico's down, and on extremely wobbly legs, feeling perilously close to tears, she left the room to tend to Lola.

CHAPTER SEVEN

RICO sat heavily on the couch once Gypsy had left. In truth his legs felt profoundly unsteady. His heart was racing and, despite the coolness he'd just projected, the taste of Gypsy, the feel of her, the scent of her, had all acted like the most powerful aphrodisiac. If they'd not been interrupted by Lola just now, he wouldn't have been far from freeing himself from his confining clothes, pulling off her jeans and surging up and into her moist heat against the window he'd just taunted her with. He burned with a need he'd only felt once before—the night he'd met her.

He reeled at realising how quickly passion had blazed—literally within minutes of arriving in the door from work. But something about the way she'd told him that she intended to leave had unleashed a wave of possessiveness and desire inside him so strong that it still astounded him.

Through the baby monitor he heard Lola's

cries abate, and Gypsy saying in a voice
that sounded suspiciously husky, 'What is it,
sweetie? You woke up?'

Even at that Rico tensed all over again, and
cursed volubly. And then the monitor went suddenly silent, as if Gypsy had realised he might
hear them and had turned it off, and he had to
restrain himself from going down to the room
and demanding irrationally that she put it back
on.

That Friday morning Gypsy got the call which
meant the inevitable end of life and freedom as
she and Lola had known it. In a curt voice Rico
wasted no time in informing her that he had the
paternity test results and they were positive.

You could have saved your precious money,
Gypsy wanted to hurl at him but didn't. She
merely listened to him tell her that he'd be home
soon to talk to her, and put down the phone.

While Mrs Wakefield gave Lola some lunch,
Gypsy paced the floor of the living room. Every
nerve in her body was coiled tight, and had been
ever since that kiss three nights ago. Since then
she'd done everything possible to avoid being
alone with Rico—much to his evident and mocking amusement. His steel-grey eyes followed her
with heavy-lidded intent whenever they were
together—which hadn't been that often, as he'd

been working till late most days, confirming for her that he would fall into a predictable pattern of work. Even that hadn't induced feelings of recrimination, only something suspiciously like disappointment.

Her motivation had changed from an intense desire to get away from Rico and his autocracy to the treacherous desire for her own self-protection. She was already so vulnerable to him, and now she was even more vulnerable. Because clearly her mind had absolutely no control over her body. And her body wanted Rico so badly that she dreamt of it when she slept and craved it when she was awake.

She hated that she could be so weak, that even knowing Rico was intent on controlling them she could still desire him so badly.

Just then she heard the unmistakable sound of his return, and went to see him standing at the door of the kitchen, taking in the sight of Lola happily chirruping away with Mrs Wakefield, causing a circle of destruction around her highchair. He had a look on his face that made Gypsy's heart twist, and then he said, sounding suspiciously gruff, 'Mrs Wakefield, I'd like to introduce you to my daughter—Lola.'

Mrs Wakefield smiled affectionately. 'Well, I could have told you that the minute I saw her. She's the image of you.'

As if just becoming aware of Gypsy's presence Rico turned his head, and all that warmth was gone in a flash. She shivered. He hated her. He really hated her now that he had incontrovertible proof that he was Lola's father.

He turned back to Mrs Wakefield and asked, 'Would you mind taking Lola for a walk when you've finished here? I have some things to discuss with Gypsy.'

The older woman said yes easily, and Rico looked back to Gypsy and said curtly, 'My study—now.'

Feeling like rebelliously stamping her foot and saying no, Gypsy took a deep quivery breath and followed his tall, broad figure down the hall and into the study. It was dark and book-lined, with all sorts of modern technology humming silently.

Rico turned and watched Gypsy enter the room, shutting the door behind her. Feeling acutely aware of her effect on him, and not liking it one bit, he sat on the edge of his desk and crossed his arms.

She looked at him with that familiar wary defiance, and a part of him felt the need to soothe, to protect and comfort. She looked incredibly young and innocent—her face clear of make-up, her hair pulled up high into a ponytail of crazy corkscrew curls that he wanted to loosen over her shoulders. But he quickly quashed the impulse.

This was what desire did to you. It clouded the ability to think straight. To see what was real. And what was real was this: Gypsy was *not* innocent. She might not be mercenary in a monetary sense, although the jury was still out on that, but she was mercenary in a far worse way as far as Rico was concerned. She would have quite happily kept Lola from him—perhaps for ever. And it was clear that she was not going to give him any straight answers. She trusted him about as much as he trusted her—that much he suspected they would agree on.

Bitter, futile anger rose *again* in acknowledgement of what he'd missed out on, but Rico pushed it down. He had to be cool, controlled. Stake his claim and leave Gypsy in no doubt as to who held the power between them.

He saw her hitch her chin up imperceptibly. 'You wanted to talk?'

He inclined his head slightly. 'As I told you earlier, I now have proof that I'm Lola's father.'

Gypsy crossed her arms across her chest, inadvertently pushing her breasts forward. Rico kept his gaze lifted with an effort, and shifted irritably on the desk.

'And…?' Gypsy asked, with all the hauteur of a queen.

Rico bit back a reluctant smile. He had to hand it to her for bravado. No one stood up to him the way she did. And he admired that, even if he didn't like admitting it.

'And that means that I am now going to exercise my rights as her father to care for her, provide for her and protect her—as befitting my heir.'

Gypsy's generous mouth tightened. 'You can do that all you want. Just let us get on with our lives and we can work out some custody arrangement.'

Rico sneered. 'You think I am going to allow you to return to that hovel of a flat with *my* daughter?' He dismissed the very notion with a slashing hand, making Gypsy flinch slightly. Perversely that made him contrite, and angry for feeling it. 'I am not interested in custody arrangements. And I am certainly not interested in being forced to stay in the UK so that I can drive into that ghetto twice a month to see my daughter for a few measly hours.'

Gypsy's arms fell, her hands clenched into fists by her sides. 'We'll take you to court. You can't do this.'

He arched a mocking brow. 'You'll take me to court with *what*? Your leftover tips from the restaurant? Believe me, Gypsy, any court you drag me to will be packed to the rafters with my own people. The best that money can buy. Do you honestly think that any judge will look favourably on a mother who wilfully cut the father of her child out of their lives for no apparent good reason? What judge will deny me my right to have access to Lola when they hear how you took it upon yourself to make her solely yours?'

He saw how she paled in the dim light, how she swayed for a moment, and with a silent curse he nearly got up to steady her. He saw her visibly compose herself. He could almost hear her brain whirring.

He decided to go for the jugular. 'You have no job. You have no prospects, despite the degree you say you have. To work you're going to need childcare, better childcare than a pensioner down the road, and to afford childcare you need to work. It's a catch-22.'

White-lipped, her green eyes huge in her face, Gypsy bit out, 'So tell me what it is you want.'

Rico relished the moment before speaking. He had Gypsy exactly where he wanted her. 'What I want is the fifteen months you owe me. You and Lola living with me for fifteen months, so that I don't miss out on another day of her development.'

This time Gypsy did sway, and Rico got to her just in time to lead her over to a chair and sit her down. In seconds he was back, with brandy in a glass. She waved it away, saying distractedly, 'Don't drink...'

He put the glass down, but stood over her and restrained himself from hauling her up and shaking her. She was acting—she had to be. This apparent vulnerability couldn't be real. And what on earth was wrong with the prospect of fifteen months living in the lap of luxury?

She looked up then, a hopeful light in her eyes. 'Fifteen months...and then you'll let us go?'

Rage bubbled inside Rico's gut. How delusional *was* she? And why did her eagerness to get away from him cause a spike in his gut? 'Not as such... But I *am* willing, after fifteen months are up, to help set you up in employment, help you find somewhere to live...help you get back on your feet. Providing, of course, that I have full and unimpeded access to Lola and a say in her future.'

Her mouth tightened again, and he could see her hands in fists on her lap.

'And in the meantime you plan on dragging us around the world with you? What kind of a life is that for a small child? She needs a routine, Rico, not a billionaire playboy father. Or are you planning to leave us in a sterile apartment like this one and visit whenever the mood strikes?'

Gypsy looked up at Rico and felt as if her neck might snap. She was so tense. His words were whirling sickeningly in her head, and along with them his obviously smug sense of satisfaction at having got her exactly where he wanted her. She needed space. She had to digest this—even though she knew with fatal certainty that what he said was true: she wouldn't have a leg to stand on in court, and had no means to get there. And, she had to acknowledge heavily, she only had herself to blame. If she hadn't taken the decision to keep Lola a secret who knew how things might have developed?

He answered her now, coldly. 'On the contrary. My main base is in Greece. I live between Athens and the island of Zakynthos. Most of my business is conducted there. This is actually my first visit back to London in…two years.'

The way he said the words, as if he was remembering that night, made the air crackle between them. Feeling claustrophobic, Gypsy blurted out before she could censor her words, 'You're not going to…to demand that we get married…?'

Rico looked down at her. He was far too close.

He arched one brow. 'Is that what you'd like, Gypsy? Is that what you're holding out for? Nothing less than matrimony?'

Before she could say that it was the last thing in the world she wanted he continued. 'Curiously, I have no desire to marry someone who believes that she has the divine right to play God with a child's life. Any wife I choose will understand the concept of honesty and trust.'

Standing up, because the feeling of claustrophobia was getting worse, and not liking they way he'd said he had no desire to marry her had impacted her somewhere very secret she bit out, 'Men like you don't even know the meaning of *trust* or *honesty*. And if I had to go back in time I'd make the same decision all over again.'

Gypsy expected Rico to move back to give her space. But he didn't. He brought his hands up to her arms and held her. Gypsy tried to pull away but his hold tightened.

Her words had hit a nerve. His eyes flashed, his jaw tightened. 'I'm not finished. I haven't told you the other thing I want.'

Gypsy's whole body was tensed against the inevitable effect of Rico's proximity. They were practically touching. All she'd have to do was take a deep breath and her breasts would push against his chest. Anger at realising that, and wanting it, made her lash out.

'*What?* Haven't you asked for enough? What more can I give you?'

He looked at her for a long moment, his steel-grey gaze intent, focused. And then he said, with devastating simplicity, '*You.*'

His words sank in, slowly, and with it came an awful trickling of heat through her veins and into her belly. She started to struggle in his arms. 'No...*no*... I won't have it. I don't want you.'

But Rico just kept on holding her and said, 'Stop lying to yourself, Gypsy.'

He brought his hands up to her face, fingers around the back of her head, holding it. His thumbs were warm on her jaw. To her utter horror she could hear her breaths coming, hard and shallow. She put her hands over his, as if she could pull them down, and entreated with everything she had, all her secret vulnerabilities where this man was concerned, 'Rico...*please* don't do this.'

He shook his head. 'I can't *not* do this.'

And with his big hands cupping her face and head, crowding her utterly, he lowered his head to hers and took her lips in a kiss of soul-destroying and surprising sweetness. As if all the tension and animosity between them was an illusion. If he'd been hard and forceful it would have been easier to remember to fight, but this… this was something else entirely.

Gypsy emitted a sound that was somewhere between a moan of capitulation and frustration. Rico urged her even closer, and she could feel him taking out her hairband and letting her hair fall, combing through it and twining long strands around his fingers. Her treacherous hands dropped.

And meanwhile his mouth was on hers, getting hotter and harder, opening her to him. He stroked his tongue along hers, enticing her to explore. And Gypsy felt her legs weaken.

In mere seconds the world shifted, and Gypsy found herself straddling Rico's lap on the chair, facing him, her legs either side of his powerful thighs. His hands were still on her head, allowing no quarter as he brought her face back to his and set about undoing every one of her defences. With a moan Gypsy had to place her hands on his chest, to stop herself falling forward completely, but that action transmitted the heavy beat of Rico's heart right through to her bones.

His hands came down to her waist, searching for and finding the bare skin between her jeans and top, stroking sensuously. Gypsy was aware that she was arching her back, but couldn't stop it. She was in another world where time and reality didn't exist. And, weakly, she resisted reality.

When Rico started to pull her T-shirt up, after only a moment of hesitation Gypsy lifted her arms and let him pull it off. Rico sat up straighter, and a new urgency infused the desire-laden air around them as he pulled her into him and pressed kisses against her neck and throat, down to the valley between her breasts.

Gypsy clutched his head, trembling all over, aching to get closer, and as if Rico heard her silent plea he shifted them subtly, so that the apex of her thighs came into direct contact with his burgeoning arousal.

She gasped and pulled back, and in that moment she realised that Rico had somehow undone her bra and was pulling it down her arms, baring her rosy-tipped breasts to his gaze.

'So beautiful...' he breathed. 'I've never for-gotten this... I've dreamt of this...'

Something about his words melted Gypsy inside, and with her hands spread on his shoul-ders all she could do was suck in a breath of pure pleasure as he cupped one breast and then brought her forward to his mouth, so that he could lick teasingly around the aureole before flicking his tongue against the hard nub.

The bare skin of her shoulders was incredibly

sensitised by her hair, and before Gypsy knew what she was doing she was blindly tearing off Rico's tie and opening the buttons of his shirt with feverish hands, all while his mouth was wickedly bringing her closer and closer to the edge of delicious sensation.

Finally, with his shirt open, Gypsy spread her hands across his broad chest with its smattering of hair, revelling in his innate strength. Rico broke away from her breast and, heavy-lidded, Gypsy looked down, her eyes roving over the stark planes of his gorgeous face, marvelling that he desired her like this. A burgeoning feeling of something awfully like tenderness rushed through her, disorientating her for a moment. It unsettled her, because she'd felt it the night they'd slept together, and finding him gone in the morning, leaving nothing but that note, had been like a slap in the face.

But he didn't give her time to dwell on that, to allow it to filter through and break the moment. Bringing her close again, he caught her mouth and kissed her until she was dizzy. One of his hands moved down over her soft belly to flick open her jeans, and she gasped open-mouthed into his kiss. His other hand came around and slid down between her jeans and her bottom, caressing the flesh, moving her in even closer, so she could feel how hard he was. In that moment he thrust upwards, and even though their clothes acted as a barrier the sheer memory of his potent size and strength made stars explode behind Gypsy's eyes.

Instinctively her hips moved, seeking more friction. He was relentless, kissing her, his hot mouth moving down, finding a breast and suckling. One hand kneaded her bottom, pulling her closer, and his other hand delved under the opening of her jeans to the apex of her legs, underneath her pants, where one finger found the moist centre of her desire and rubbed, back and forth, as he rhythmically thrust against her.

Almost sobbing, because on some level Gypsy knew that he was only displaying his control over her, showing her how weak she was, she couldn't save herself from the ultimate surrender. With a cry, she felt her body tense and peak, before falling down into spasms of pleasure so intense that her hands dug into Rico's shoulders as if he was her anchor in the storm.

To her absolute horror, as sanity came back in slow doses, she could feel her body still clenching spasmodically. She was half naked, *in his study*, and had just been brought to orgasm for the first time in two years with little more than heavy petting.

On roiling waves of shock and horror Gypsy pulled Rico's hands away and scrambled up.

Her jeans were undone, half off. Her breasts throbbed, her body ached—and Rico sat there, sprawled in sexy abandon, with his shirt open and his hair dishevelled.

She saw her T-shirt and whipped it up, pulling it on with shaking hands, not caring if it was back to front or inside out. Or where her bra was. With a strangled cry of something she couldn't even articulate she fled from the study.

All she heard behind her was a dark, knowing chuckle.

Fleeing straight to her bedroom, Gypsy locked herself in the bathroom, turned the shower onto steaming, stripped and got in. Only once she was under the powerful spray did she give in to tears of humiliation and anger. Rico had proved his point. He held all the power—over her situation, over Lola, and—possibly worst of all—*over her.* Because if she couldn't remain immune to Rico how could she protect herself or Lola, when inevitably he would lose interest in being a father and reject them both?

When she felt composed and had changed into a polo-neck top and fresh jeans, Gypsy wound her damp hair up and stuck a clip in it. Taking a deep breath, she went back out to the living room—where, to her dismay, she saw Rico standing looking out of the window. No sign of Mrs Wakefield or Lola yet.

Rico turned to face her, hands in his pockets, and Gypsy cursed the fact that he hadn't gone back to work—knowing that it was hypocritical of her, because if he had she'd have found fault with that too. Looking as cool as a cucumber, and not as if he'd just made love to her within an inch of her life on a chair in his study, Rico held out a piece of paper to Gypsy.

She had to go closer to get it, and all but snatched it out of his hand. She glanced at him before reading it. 'What's this?'

'It's a press release.'

Gypsy read the print.

After a break in relations, Rico Christofides and Gypsy Butler would like to announce their joyful reunion, together with their daughter Lola.

She looked up from the paper and felt shaky all over. 'Is this really necessary?'

He nodded curtly. 'Absolutely. They will dig and dig until they know who you are, who Lola is, and what her relationship to me is. We give them that, and a staged photo, and they'll leave us alone…'

Gypsy could feel her blood drain southwards,

and was barely aware of Rico's narrowed look. 'They won't dig if we give them this?'

His look was far too assessing, and Gypsy tried to hide her fear of people finding out about her past, terrified that Rico would use the knowledge in some way to strengthen his position. He shook his head. 'No, they'll still hound us to a certain extent, but it won't have the same intensity…'

Gypsy handed him back the paper. 'OK, then, go ahead with it.'

Rico said smoothly, 'I already have.'

Gypsy's eyes clashed with his. 'Of course. How could I forget? You act and then ask later.'

Rico shrugged nonchalantly. 'I know what I want and I go after it. Now,' he said crisply, and looked at his watch, 'my driver is downstairs, waiting to take you to your flat, where you will pack up the rest of your things. Bring back only what you can carry. I'll have my assistant box everything else up and ship it to my home in Athens.'

'But what about the flat?'

Rico's lip curled. 'My assistant will look after informing the landlord. No doubt it'll soon be snapped up by the next unfortunate individual who has to live there.'

Gypsy bit back words of protest, knowing they were futile. 'Then what?'

'Then…' Rico came close to Gypsy, but she backed away, not liking the way butterflies took off in her belly. 'Tomorrow we travel to Buenos Aires for my nephew's christening, which is in a few days. I'm to be his godfather. I also have some business to attend to while we're there.'

Intrigued despite herself, Gypsy asked, 'You have a nephew?'

'He's my younger half-brother's son.' Almost accusingly he said, 'Lola has cousins: four-year-old Beatriz and six-month-old Luis. My brother Rafael and his wife Isobel are looking forward to meeting you and Lola.'

Gypsy felt a little overwhelmed to suddenly discover that he had family—that he was going to be a godfather and that Lola had cousins. It made her feel a curious wrenching inside. *Family*. Lola might never have known. It was something Gypsy had always longed for—a brother or sister, even cousins. But both her parents had been only children, and she'd been her father's only child.

In something of a daze, she let Rico guide her out to the hall. She put on her coat and went down to the car. All the way to her flat, and as she packed up her paltry belongings, Gypsy was still in a bit of a daze. Finally she looked around and heaved a sigh. The flat looked even worse now that she'd been living in Rico's penthouse for a week. Even she couldn't stomach the thought of bringing Lola back here…

She looked down and made sure she had her most important possession: an old box full of mementos of her mother—photos, and those letters she'd found in her father's study after he'd died. She didn't care about anything else.

She sat down heavily on a chair for a moment, feeling emotion welling within her, but she stayed dry-eyed and just felt inexplicably sad and fearful that despite everything she was destined to watch as Lola received the same treatment she'd got from her own father.

And yet Gypsy had to acknowledge the utter shock Rico must have felt to find out about Lola. But from that first moment he'd taken it on board and assumed Lola was his. At no point had he rejected her, or ignored her until he'd got the results of the paternity test back. She had to admit grudgingly, for the second time in the space of a few days, that in spite of his autocratic takeover of their lives he hadn't been acting exactly as she'd feared.

Gypsy had borne little physical resemblance to her father, and he too had insisted on a DNA test once he'd been forced to take her in—even though he'd known of her existence. With the proof that she was his, he'd just looked at her, shaken his head, and said, 'It'd be easier to look at you if you at least took after the Bastions... but there's nothing. You're all your poor, stupid, mad Irish mother—and with that hair you look just like the gypsies she named you after...'

Gypsy blinked back the memory, her focus returning to the room. In a way, she thought, at least Lola *did* resemble Rico. That must be why it was easier for him to bond with her.

With a last desultory look around, she stood up, picking up the bags. Making sure she had the box, she left the flat for the last time. On her way back to the penthouse, the prospect of facing Rico and the future he'd outlined for them made the emotions clamouring in her chest feel much more ambiguous than she liked to admit.

The following day, after they'd arrived at a private airfield and been shown onto a plush private plane, Gypsy thought back to that morning. In a hive of activity, while getting ready for the trip to Argentina, Rico had reminded her of completing the necessary paperwork to have him added to Lola's birth certificate.

Then he'd curtly informed her, 'The paparazzi are outside waiting. They know they're going to get a shot of us leaving, so I'd appreciate it if you could bring yourself to wear some of the clothes I bought for you. Also, in Buenos Aires there are a couple of functions I have to attend—not to mention the christening…'

In other words, Gypsy had surmised as she'd packed angrily, leaving behind her own shabby clothes, she'd better dress the part from now on. And he was also informing her that he expected her to be at his side in public…

She turned to him now on the plane, as she held Lola on her lap as they took off, but he was engrossed in some paperwork, giving her his slightly crooked profile, which only made him look more dangerous.

Stifling a sigh, Gypsy looked out of the window as England dropped away below them and felt as though a net was tightening around her, slowly but surely.

A couple of hours into the flight, after Lola had exhausted the length and breadth of the plane, and had been fed and changed, she was asleep on one of the reclined seats near Gypsy, the seat belt tied securely over her blanket, thumb stuck firmly in her mouth.

Gypsy looked from Lola to Rico, and flushed when she caught him staring at her. She blurted out what had been on her mind earlier. 'Are you suggesting that we appear in public together… like some sort of…couple?'

His eyes narrowed. 'I've released a press statement to the effect that we are...*together*, so, yes, I am going to make full use of you by my side. I need a companion in public, and of late have not had anyone to fulfil that role.'

Gypsy's heart beat fast, and to counteract it she said waspishly, 'The redhead wasn't fit for public duty?'

Rico smiled, and it made him look years younger, more carefree... *Lord*, thought Gypsy, remembering when he'd smiled at her like that the night they met.

'You're inordinately interested in this redhead.'

Gypsy snorted inelegantly, but couldn't look away. *Had* he slept with her? She hated that she wanted to know, and that she cared. She balled her hands into fists, nails scoring her palms.

'I'm not interested in the slightest,' she lied. 'I would just like to know what the public perception of my role is likely to be if I'm to be seen by your side.'

'I'd say it's likely to be that you are the mother of my child, who is also sharing my bed. And if it's any consolation I didn't sleep with the redhead that night; seeing you again rendered me all but impotent.'

Gypsy flushed and struggled to control her

wayward response to hearing that admission. She asserted hotly, 'I will *not* be sharing your bed.'

He shrugged, and released her from his gaze to look back to his work, then said, 'We both know if I started kissing you I could have you on the bed in the back of this cabin within minutes... But with respect to our daughter I'll desist from making my point here and now.'

Gypsy choked back something rude...but couldn't for the life of her stop her mind from imagining Rico coming over to her seat, trapping her with his arms and bending down to kiss her, before lifting her up and carrying her to the back of the plane...to that bed...where all she could imagine was a tangle of limbs, olive skin contrasting with pale skin...

What was wrong with her? Gypsy opened her belt and got up to go to the bathroom. Only once she was locked inside, and after splashing cold water on her face, did her pulse finally return to something close to normal. She looked at her face in the mirror, eyes huge. She was terrified that sleeping with Rico would crumble her precious defences...he already had so much control—too much control. If he had *her*, then he would have it all.

She'd been too young to fight against her father's control, and he'd tried to wipe away every last trace of who she really was. She couldn't forget that. She had to fight Rico for her own preservation and Lola's. She *had* to.

Gypsy woke to a gentle prodding, and opened her eyes to see Lola's big grey ones staring up at her, alongside Rico's. He was squatting by her side, holding her. She was awake in an instant, her back protesting as she'd fallen asleep sitting up.

Lola smiled at her, small teeth flashing, 'Mama…fly!'

Gypsy smiled tightly, hiding her momentary sense of disorientation at knowing that Rico had obviously taken care of Lola when she'd woken, and had been watching her sleeping. Lola was picking up more and more words every day now, generally repeating back any words said to her. Gypsy automatically went to reach for her, but Rico took her over to sit on his lap. Gypsy saw that his paperwork was put away.

He glanced at her and said, 'We're landing shortly. Buckle up.'

And just like that he was settling a completely contented Lola in his arms, and securing the seat belt around them. It made her think again of how at ease he'd been with Lola from day one. And he was growing in confidence around her, having no apparent qualms about picking her up or playing with her. He'd shielded her from the glare of the paprazzi cameras as they'd left the penthouse that morning, cocooning her within his arms. This side of Rico was one she hadn't anticipated, and while she still didn't doubt it was temporary, while the novelty lasted it unsettled her more than she liked to admit.

She couldn't help asking curiously, 'Have you always wanted children?'

Rico sent her a quick look, his hands huge around Lola, making something ache in Gypsy's chest. She qualified. 'That is…you seem very comfortable with Lola…'

Rico felt his daughter's plump and solid little body curved into him so trustingly, and knew without a moment's hesitation that he would lay his life down for her. Gypsy was looking at him with those huge eyes, her hair tumbled around her shoulders in glorious abandon. Her question unsettled him. He'd never thought about having children—had never wanted to have children. How could he explain that the concept of fatherhood had always mystified him, having had no good experience to call on?

But the day he'd seen Lola for the first time he'd suddenly *known* instinctively what it was. And as he'd come to terms with it, he had been able to feel so much more of his father's pain and loss. And also to hate his stepfather even more for his cruel treatment. And…a hardness settled in his chest…he could also hate Gypsy a little bit more for denying him this basic right.

But he couldn't articulate this to the woman who sat across from him, the woman he'd found himself staring at while she slept, looking so innocent. It had taken all his restraint and control not to pick her up out of her seat and carry her down to the bedroom to slake his lust. He hated wanting her so badly. He wanted to be able to control his desire. He wanted to be immune to her charms, unmoved by her wild beauty which called to him as strongly now as when he'd first seen her.

He schooled his features, afraid she might see something of the turmoil within him. 'Whether I wanted children or not is no longer a relevant question. I have Lola, and the reason I'm comfortable with her is because she is *mine*, my flesh and blood, and I will do everything in my power to protect her.'

CHAPTER EIGHT

THE fervour of Rico's words still rang in Gypsy's head as they sped along the wide Buenos Aires boulevards to Rico's brother's home, where they were going to be guests. A trickle of sweat dropped between her breasts even though the car was air-conditioned. It had been like walking into a baking oven, stepping off the plane into the bright Argentinian sunshine just a short while before.

Rico had warned Gypsy how hot it was likely to be, but even in light linen trousers and a shirt she was still hot. Luckily there had been some summer dresses and light clothes amongst Lola's new wardrobe, and now she was all decked out in a gorgeous polka dot dress, complete with sandals and matching pants.

Sitting in a baby seat, she looked out at the view with big eyes, turning to smile winningly at Gypsy every now and then, or to point and exclaim intermittently, 'Car!' or, 'Woof! Woof!' when she saw a dog.

Rico was sitting in the front, alongside the driver, conversing in Spanish. He looked back at Lola indulgently when she pointed out the umpteenth car. 'Very good, *mi nenita*...'

Gypsy had to swallow an inexplicable lump, and looked out of her own window. She wondered if there would come a time when Rico might look at *her* without that censorious, unforgiving light in his eyes, and despaired that she even wanted that.

She could see that they were in a more residential area now, with huge houses just visible behind tall trees and flowering bushes. The car slowed, and a set of ornate black gates opened to reveal a long drive which led to a huge open courtyard and a stunning house.

On the steps Gypsy could see a beautiful slim woman with short dark hair holding a chubby black-haired baby, and beside her a tall dark man who bore a striking resemblance to Rico. It had to be Rafael—his half-brother. And between their legs danced a small dark-haired girl in worn shorts and a T-shirt, bare feet. The sight comforted Gypsy, who hadn't really known what to expect.

They got out. Gypsy was all fingers and thumbs on Lola's straps, but finally managed to extricate her. She went shy at the sight of so many new faces and leant into Gypsy, her thumb in her mouth.

Rico was by her side then, a hand on her back, and Gypsy felt slightly comforted. They walked forward, and any trepidation fled at the huge smile on Rafael's wife's face as she walked forward to meet them, embracing Gypsy warmly, and then Rico.

'It's *so* lovely to meet you, Gypsy. And Lola—isn't she a sweetie?' Gypsy was surprised to hear that Isobel sounded quite English, and also *looked* more English than Argentinian.

Gypsy was aware of the two brothers greeting each other warmly, but with a certain reserve she couldn't put her finger on. She smiled at Rafael in greeting, and could see that up close there were distinct similarities. But where Rico's eyes were that cold steel-grey, Rafael's were dark brown. And he didn't have the air of suppressed danger that seemed to surround Rico like a cloak of darkness.

The introductions were quick and chaotic. Beatriz their four-year-old daughter, was adorable, with big chocolate-brown eyes, and clearly excited to meet her new cousin.

Rico surprised Gypsy by picking Beatriz up and making her squeal with delight, before saying, 'Once Lola is settled in you can get to know her…'

Beatriz smiled and said, 'OK, Uncle Rico.'

In a flurry of being ushered inside, where a homely housekeeper appeared, wiping her hands on an apron, and more introductions, Gypsy deduced that Rafael and Isobel were blissfully happy. It oozed from every cell of their beings and throughout the house as Isobel led Gypsy on a whirlwind tour.

Standing at a bedroom door some minutes later, Isobel apologised, saying with a grimace, 'I'm sorry—you must be absolutely exhausted. I know how arduous the flight can be from England; I went to school there, near my father's family. But here I am chattering on when all you probably want to do is wash and rest.'

Isobel was cradling her smiley baby easily, and Gypsy felt in that moment that they could be good friends. She'd never had a close female friend before. She smiled shyly, feeling a sudden weariness wash over her. 'To be honest, it's all been a bit of a whirlwind…but I'm very happy to meet you too—and your children are gorgeous.'

Isobel grimaced again, but smiled. '*Most* of the time, as I'm sure you well know.'

Gypsy shared a complicit smile and appreciated Isobel's lack of questions when she and

Rafael had to have dozens. Just then Rico appeared, and Isobel gestured to the huge luxuriously furnished room through the open door. 'I hope this will be suitable for you both, and Lola. I've set up a cot for Lola in the room off the dressing room, so she's close by. I've also left baby monitors in there if you want them at night. If you need anything else just shout. Someone will bring your bags up shortly, but get some rest in the meantime. We'll eat at about eight, after the children are in bed.'

Rico's voice rumbled through Gypsy. 'Thank you, Isobel, we'll see you later.'

With a little wave Isobel walked quickly down the corridor. Gypsy and Rico still stood at the bedroom door. With a hand on her back he propelled her inside. Gypsy clutched Lola to her like a lifeline as she realised something very scary on investigating the rooms. One bedroom, one bathroom, one dressing room and one smaller room, where a cot and changing table had been set up.

She whirled to face Rico. 'This room is surely for me and Lola. Where's your room?'

He crossed his arms. 'Right here.'

Gypsy backed away and shook her head. Rico had changed on the plane, into a pair of faded denims and a dark polo shirt, and he was all too devastating to her equilibrium like this. 'No way. We are not sharing a bed. Obviously Isobel has assumed we're a…a couple. I'll have to let her know.'

Gypsy walked purposefully forward, but Rico stopped her with his arm. Lola, the little traitor, squirmed out of Gypsy's arms towards Rico, and she had to let her go when he reached for her. Looking far too smug, he said, 'You will do no such thing. She's gone to a lot of trouble to set this room up, and would be mortified to think that you're not happy with the arrangement.'

He shrugged insouciantly. 'All we have to do is share a king-sized bed. You can put pillows down the centre, if you like. Or is it that you're just afraid that you won't be able to help yourself from ripping my clothes off?'

Gypsy balled her hands into fists and felt another trickle of sweat go down the small of her back. 'You're just playing with me. You can't seriously expect me to believe that there aren't a dozen more bedrooms here that you could use.'

'It's not up for debate, Gypsy. Now, you can go and bother Isobel with this tiny problem, when she's got her hands full with her kids and organising the christening in two days, or you can just let it go and be an adult about it.'

Once again Gypsy felt like stamping her foot. What was it about this man that made her regress to a mental age of fifteen? But steel resolve straightened her spine. 'Fine. If that's the way you want it, I will have no problem keeping my hands off you. But know this, Rico Christofides, if you so much as breathe near me I will scream this place down.'

Rico smiled a shark's smile. 'You might scream, but it won't be to keep me away from you.'

Gypsy flushed, remembering how abandoned she'd been the night they'd slept together. And the other day in the study. No self-control whatsoever. Mortified, and burning up inside with humiliation but determined not to let him see it, she held out her hands for Lola, who just looked at her, quite content in Rico's arms. 'I should feed her now. She'll be hungry.'

Rico said easily, 'Why don't I feed her and let you wash and rest? I'll bring her back up when she's ready to go down for the evening. Beatriz is probably driving her parents crazy wanting to see her again anyway.'

And just like that he took responsibility for her daughter. Feeling thoroughly disgruntled and at odds with everything, her emotions seesawing wildly, Gypsy could only watch as Rico walked out with Lola high in his arms, chattering away happily.

Still muttering to herself, Gypsy had a brief

shower, and when she emerged in a voluminous fluffy robe, feeling half-human again, there was a smiling girl putting away their clothes. *Their clothes: hers and Rico's.* That curious ache settled in her chest again, and Gypsy stuttered her thanks as the girl melted away discreetly.

The bed looked both terrifying and more inviting than anything she'd ever seen and, feeling as if surely she could snatch ten minutes of a nap, Gypsy lay down.

She woke much later, when dusk had fallen outside, to the familiar sound of Lola's cry. Instantly she was awake, and saw Rico come into the room with an obviously cranky Lola in his arms. When she saw Gypsy she started to wail even louder. For the first time since she'd met him again Rico didn't look his assured self. He actually looked *worried*.

Gypsy pulled her robe tight around her, wishing she had taken the time to dress, and took Lola, whose wails decreased almost immediately.

Rico said tightly, 'I'm not sure what's wrong with her. She ate some lunch and played with Beatriz, and then suddenly she started crying…'

Gypsy knew it would be all too easy to make Rico feel bad, but that knowledge didn't sit well. She couldn't do it. She looked at him, trying not to notice how gorgeous he seemed in the dim light of the room, in the intimacy of this situation like any domestic couple with their child.

Smiling wryly, she said, 'Welcome to cranky and tired Lola. She can go from upbeat and happy to heartbroken in an instant. It's been a lot for her to take in today, that's all. She just needs to wind down and get to bed… I'll get her a bottle and put her down.'

Rico surprised her by saying he'd get the bottle, and while he was gone Gypsy bathed Lola and changed her for the night. She couldn't help sensing his relief at knowing that he hadn't been at fault for upsetting Lola and that she was OK.

When he came back Gypsy was rocking Lola back and forth. She took the bottle from Rico and, after testing it, gave it to Lola, who was already falling asleep after a few greedy gulps. Rico stood with a shoulder against the doorjamb, watching them, and Gypsy felt huge relief at escaping from his intense scrutiny when she put Lola down and those long-lashed eyes closed in exhaustion.

She came out of the small room and pulled the door partway closed behind her, making sure to leave the baby monitor on in the room.

Rico said, 'I'll have a shower and see you

downstairs, if you like. Dinner will be ready soon.'

Gypsy nodded, and as soon as she heard the shower going raced out of the robe and into a plain black dress and slingback heels, tying her hair back at her nape to tame it as much as she could. Escaping downstairs before Rico might emerge with just a towel around his waist seemed like the most important thing in the world.

She'd taken the second baby monitor with her, and as she approached the reception area a maid appeared as if from thin air and showed Gypsy into the main drawing room. Gypsy blushed to the roots of her hair when she saw Isobel sitting on Rafael's lap, their heads close together, his arms about her waist, her arms around his neck.

Isobel jumped up the minute she saw her, an impish grin on her face. 'I'm sorry, Gypsy, we didn't see you... Would you like an aperitif?'

Rafael stood too, and greeted Gypsy so urbanely that he defused her embarrassment. By the time Rico appeared, in a snowy-white shirt and black trousers, Gypsy was explaining to Rafael and Isobel about her name. As soon as Rico came and stood near her, though, her voice dried up in her throat at imagining sharing a bed with him that night.

The housekeeper appeared and called them through for dinner, which was served in a wood-panelled dining room.

Gypsy sat back after the dessert and patted her belly, trying to ignore Rico's steely gaze across the table. She looked at Isobel. 'That was too delicious for words...'

Isobel smiled. She was sitting directly opposite Gypsy, to Rafael's right, with Rico beside her at the head of the table. 'It's nice that it's just us this evening. I understand that you're going to a function tomorrow night and that's lucky for you as you'll get to avoid the arrival of our other guests and the ensuing mayhem of preparations for the christening.'

Instinctively Gypsy leant forward. 'Is there anything I can do to help?'

Isobel waved a hand. 'Not at all. It's all in hand. Believe me, it's just lovely that you're here.' She sent a mischievous look to Rico. 'According to Rico, we should never have believed that he might one day appear with a ready-made family.' She continued. 'What was it you said on our wedding day? Something about not offering a return invitation any time soon?'

Rico looked steadily at Gypsy and she was caught by his gaze, unable to read it or escape it. A muscle ticked in his jaw, and then he drawled, 'Well...since I can't remember issuing a proposal, I'd say what I said then still holds firm...'

Gypsy was only vaguely aware of Rafael's sharp intake of breath, and the discreet look between him and Isobel. Gypsy burned inside with humiliation, which was made worse because she knew his statement *shouldn't* bother her—especially not after he'd succinctly outlined his requirements for a wife. But before she could come back with some witty rejoinder, to show how he hadn't affected her even when he *had*, the door opened and Rafael and Isobel's nanny came in.

She said something to Isobel, who stood up, apologising. 'It's Luis. He won't settle. Please excuse me?'

Wanting desperately to escape, Gypsy half stood and said, 'I should check on Lola.' But to her dismay Isobel waved her back down. 'Don't be silly. Have your coffee and I'll check on her for you.'

Feeling sick inside, Gypsy sat back down and couldn't meet Rico's eye. Thankfully Rafael seemed happy to cover the gap in conversation, and Gypsy let the talk flow over her. She hated that she felt so hurt by Rico's comment. He'd all but stated that he wouldn't be marrying Gypsy if she was the last woman on earth, even if she was the mother of his child. And she didn't even *want* to marry him! He was welcome to the tall, sleek, blonde heiress-type he'd undoubtedly go for. Or the sultry redhead—even if he said he hadn't slept with her.

After what she deemed an appropriate amount of time she excused herself, saying to Rafael, 'The jet lag is catching up with me. If you don't mind, I think I'll go to bed.'

Praying that Rico wouldn't follow her, she breathed a sigh of relief when she heard Rafael continue the conversation. She all but ran up the stairs, and practically bumped into Isobel, who was coming back down.

Isobel touched Gypsy's arm and asked gently, 'Are you OK?'

Gypsy nodded. She felt like bursting into tears, but held it back.

Isobel bit her lip and said, 'I didn't mean to say anything to cause tension between you and Rico. I'm so sorry... I saw the way he was with you, and I guess I just assumed...'

She looked so mournful that Gypsy blocked out her pathetic need to know what Isobel meant by *I saw the way he was with you* and shook her head. 'No, it's not you at all. Believe me. It's just...things aren't exactly how they seem with me and Rico...we're not...*together.*'

Isobel groaned. 'And I put you two in the same room. I am *so* sorry. Look, I'll move Rico—'

'No!' Gypsy said forcibly, anticipating Rico's retribution, and forced herself to say calmly, 'Don't—really. It's fine, honestly. Our relationship is not to be a cause of concern to you.'

Isobel took Gypsy's arm and walked her back down the corridor towards the bedrooms. 'If it's any consolation, I think I might know a little of what you're going through…' she confided.

Gypsy frowned. 'But you and Rafael seem so…' She trailed off, remembering intruding on their intimate moment.

Isobel smiled ruefully. 'Oh, we are *now*. But, believe me, it wasn't always like that.' She shook her head, 'Considering their background, and the damage their father—' She stopped and clarified. 'That is the damage Rafael's father, Rico's stepfather, did to them both, it's easy to see where they get their drive and arrogance. And Rico had it so much worse than Rafael, because he was someone else's son. Rafael doesn't even know what happened between Rico and his biological father when he left at sixteen to go and find him in Greece.'

Reeling inwardly at this information, Gypsy repeated, 'He left at sixteen?'

Isobel nodded. 'After a beating that nearly put him in a hospital. If he hadn't turned on his stepfather that day and fought back, who knows what might have happened? As it was, he saved

Rafael from years of further abuse...' Isobel turned to Gypsy at the door of the bedroom. 'Look, if there's any way I can make this more comfortable for you, let me know.'

Gypsy forced a smile. 'I will. And thank you.'

Isobel hugged Gypsy impulsively before walking away.

When Gypsy had let herself into the bedroom she stood with her back to the door for a long moment while silent tears slid down her cheeks. The other woman's easy affection had pushed her over the edge of her control.

She wiped at the tears that wouldn't seem to stop and told herself angrily that she *wasn't* crying at the thought of a proud sixteen-year-old being beaten so badly that he'd left home. She'd already begun to suspect that Rico was a much more complex person than her father. Hearing that intriguing snippet about his and Rafael's childhood made her want to know more, and that was dangerous. Along with the ever-increasing proof that when it came to *his* daughter he was proving to be nothing like her own father.

He was making Gypsy pay, yes, just as her father had done to her mother—but not because she'd asked him to acknowledge Lola, but because she *hadn't*.

And while his words tonight should have comforted her, telling her of his intention that they would never formalise their relationship just for the sake of their daughter or because he might gain more control over them, they had done anything but. The words had scored through her like a serrated knife.

Suddenly anticipating Rico striding into the room, Gypsy hurriedly dressed in her night-clothes and got into bed, hugging one side. She put a pillow in the centre as a warning to Rico, but she had no doubt after that comment down-stairs that he'd be as likely to try and seduce her as he would be to give Lola up.

Rico came into the room and saw the slight shape under the covers in the bed. A small bedside light threw out a dim glow, and Rico walked over to look down on Gypsy where she lay sleeping. He cursed softly when he saw the unmistakable sign of tear-tracks on her cheeks, feeling his chest tighten. He did not welcome the unbidden emotion where this woman was concerned.

Dammit. He'd just had to endure the worst look of reproach from Isobel, and Rafael's clear disapproval. He hadn't told them, however, that he had regretted the words as soon as they'd come out of his mouth. He'd wanted to snatch them back as soon as he'd seen the colour leach from Gypsy's face and her eyes grow bruised. It had been a cheap shot designed to hurt, and it had.

Rico was disconcerted by this need to hurt Gypsy, because it hinted at a desire to force her to push him away. When really he knew he didn't have to make much of an effort there. He was surprised she hadn't hit him the other day, after he'd seduced her in his study and all but exploded like an inexperienced teenager in his pants. What had started out as an exercise in domination over her had turned rapidly into something completely out of his control.

Gypsy hated him, but perversely that thought didn't give him the same satisfaction it might have a few days ago. His mouth thinned. He had done something or he represented something that she despised. It was becoming more and more clear that something lay behind her reasoning for not getting in touch with him when she'd found out about her pregnancy.

She kept making comments about *men like you*, or *I know how you operate*, and it was beginning to seriously get on his nerves. And yet she'd had an opportunity earlier to make the most of his discomfiture when he hadn't known how to deal with Lola's bad behaviour, but she hadn't. She'd been generous and had put him at ease, assuring him it wasn't his fault.

And he'd repaid her by making a snide comment.

He was used to people looking for a weakness and exploiting it, and she hadn't done that. She was full of shadows and secrets which he was only now beginning to unravel. She didn't trust him, she didn't want his money, and she fought her attraction to him as if her life depended on it. And he wanted to know why. Right at that moment, despite the most urgent desire he'd ever felt for a woman burning him up inside, he felt the need to proceed cautiously, suddenly wary of what further vulnerabilities intimacy might bring.

'I owe you an apology.'

Gypsy's hand tightened around her coffee cup. It was just her and Rico in the bright and airy breakfast room. When she'd woken this morning she'd been inordinately relieved to find Rico's side of the bed empty. He'd already taken Lola downstairs to eat with Beatriz, Isobel and Luis, and Isobel had insisted on taking Lola off to play with Beatriz.

So now it was just the two of them, and she had to have misheard. She looked at him warily. 'Apology?'

He nodded once, curtly, the lines of his clean-shaven face stark. 'What I said last night was unforgivably rude. You are the mother of my child and deserve more respect.'

If Gypsy hadn't already been sitting down she would have fallen. She got the distinct impression that those words had cost him dearly. She might be the mother of his child but he still despised her for what she had done. But then her heart thumped—was he saying that he *would* marry her? She went hot all over, and clammy at the same time.

As if Rico could see the direction of her thoughts he said mockingly, 'While I don't envisage such a union between us, I had no right to say it so baldly. Suffice to say, I still don't relish the thought of marrying a woman who thinks nothing of keeping the father out of his child's life.'

Gypsy's chin hitched up. So he was apologising not for what he'd said, but how he'd said it. Fresh hurt lanced her, mocking her attempt to deny it. 'I didn't think *nothing* of it. I had my reasons and they were good ones.'

Rico leant forward, suddenly threatening. 'Yes, about those reasons… You've not been entirely forthcoming in that area. You're determined to believe the worst of me—that's been clear since the moment we met again—and you've obviously thought the worst since you knew who I was. That's why you never contacted me, isn't it? While I find it hard to believe, I'm willing to bet that you slept with me that night because you truly *did* think I was just some anonymous person, and not one of the wealthiest men in the world.' He said this with no arrogance, just stated the fact.

Gypsy's skin tightened across her bones and she confirmed his suspicion, saying faintly, 'I didn't know anything about you till I saw you on the news that morning...'

Her brain whirred sickeningly. He was issuing a direct challenge and skirting far too close to the truth. He couldn't know about her father; he couldn't know the dramatic step she'd taken after he had died. If he shared the antipathy her father had felt for him, he'd use that for sure. And he couldn't know about her mother's mental instability. He wouldn't understand—few people would—and he would use all that information to make her appear an unfit mother.

She was aware on some level that this fear was coming from a visceral place, not necessarily rational, but she couldn't control it. She didn't see herself ever being able to trust Rico. She couldn't remember the last time she'd trusted anyone.

How could she, when her formative experiences had been learnt so painfully at the hands of someone who hadn't even been as powerful?

She reiterated. 'As I told you before, I had no desire to be dragged through the courts, and your departure that morning had left me in no doubt as to how reluctant you were to see me again.'

He seemed to consider saying something for a long time, and eventually he said roughly, 'I told you the day I came to your flat that I regretted leaving you the way I did.'

Gypsy swallowed. She'd dismissed his words as an easy platitude at the time, but now they skated over her skin and made little tremors race up and down.

His mouth tightened into a thin line. 'I rang the hotel…most likely just after you would have seen me on the news…but you'd already left…'

Gypsy stopped breathing. She had the vaguest recollection of a phone ringing as she'd walked away from the room, but she had assumed it was coming from somewhere else. That had been *him*? To say what? That he wanted to see her again? But even as she thought that, and her heart clenched treacherously, she realised that she'd known who he was by then…so she would still have run, disgusted at having let herself be seduced so easily by someone like him.

She'd still been raw after her father's death—especially as she'd just found out the extent of his cruelty to her mother.

Gypsy tore her eyes from his and looked down, feeling very wobbly inside. 'You say that you rang. Whether you did or not is a moot point now.'

'Clearly.'

Rico's voice was harsh enough to have Gypsy's eyes meet his, and something in those grey depths made her breath hitch.

And then, moving abruptly, Rico put down his napkin and stood up. 'I have to go into my office here today. The event we're going to tonight is black tie—it's for a charity I'm patron of. Be ready to go out at seven p.m.'

Gypsy watched as Rico strode powerfully from the room, and when he'd gone the absence of his intense energy made her sag like a lead balloon. She'd been to dozens of society charity events, as her father had been patron of many—but only to enhance his ego, avail himself of tax benefits, and occasionally to dip into the funds for himself.

He'd never got caught. He'd been too good at creating smoke and mirrors so people didn't ask questions or looked the other way. But Gypsy had known, though she'd always been too terrified of the potential punishment if she did something as audacious as call the police. But nevertheless her father had managed to punish her for her knowledge.

Once again she was being hurtled back in time. With effort she forced her mind away. She'd never wanted to be party to something like this again, and here she was, right in the middle of it. She let familiar cynicism wash over her as she thought of the prospect of the evening to come, but knew it was a weak attempt to avoid the thought of going out on Rico's arm in public.

She couldn't even drum up the disgust she'd expected to feel at the thought of seeing Rico posture and preen purely to raise his profile. She had an uncomfortable presentiment that he would confound her expectations again.

That evening Gypsy sat beside Rico at the head table, in a thronged and glittering ballroom in one of Buenos Aires' best hotels. She was incensed that her distaste for this milieu was being constantly diminished because she was so distracted by how gorgeous Rico looked in a classic black-tie tuxedo.

Isobel was minding Lola, and had kindly helped Gypsy to get ready earlier. She'd endeared herself to Gypsy even more when she'd confided with feeling that she and Rafael had a pact that they'd only go to charity events if and when it was absolutely necessary, and only if Rafael could promise that he would try to extort as much money as possible out of the assembled Buenos Aires elite. After they'd given over their own generous donation, of course.

Gypsy had been happy with her appearance once Isobel had left. Her hair was straightened and twisted into a classic chignon, and her plain dark green silk dress, sleeveless and with a cowl neckline, fell to the floor. She looked the part—the part she'd been trained well to play by her own father when it had suited him to act out the role of devoted parent, which had only ever lasted as long as they'd been on public display.

When Rico had come into the bedroom earlier and asked, with a horrified glance at her head, 'What have you done to your hair?' Gypsy had felt like a gauche teenager again—acutely self-conscious and aware that she just didn't have the right *look* for this world.

Defensively she'd touched her hair and said, 'Isobel straightened it for me. It's tidier like this… I thought for the dinner—'

But he'd just said curtly, 'Come on, we'll be late,' and strode out of the room, making Gypsy want to slam and lock the door behind him.

Now she looked resolutely away from Rico, and tried not to let the fact that his powerful thigh was brushing against hers intermittently bother her. But she couldn't pretend to herself that she wasn't affected, and squirmed inwardly at the thought of Rico knowing.

Suddenly a hush descended on the room as a compère got up and signalled to the crowd. She heard Rico sigh deeply beside her and snuck a look. His face was expressionless, but his jaw was tight, and she knew in that instant that he too hated this. Reeling at that information, she watched dumbly as he got up with fluid athletic grace after being introduced, and walked to the podium with thunderous adoring applause resounding around the room.

Up until that point Gypsy hadn't taken much notice of what the charity in question was, but now she recognised it as one of her father's own pet projects. One that he'd taken funds from. Her face burned with mortification at the realisation, and also at the weak fear that had led her to keep quiet about it when she'd been younger.

Rico was talking now, and Gypsy became quickly mesmerised by the simple articulacy of his words and his obvious genuine passion for the cause. A few people shifted uncomfortably around her; clearly they'd just expected him to get up and smile and say nothing of any consequence. But Rico was not going anywhere yet.

He knew his subject well. He was listing facts

and figures that made her feel dizzy, and he was not afraid of mentioning the unpalatable stuff that people at an event like this preferred not to hear. To her knowledge he hadn't even brought a piece of paper, but with simple eloquence he put it to the crowd to put their money where their mouths were and started an impromptu bidding session—the prize being a new car of the winner's choice, from him. She could see exactly what he'd done; he'd embarrassed them into action, and now they couldn't bid fast enough.

The woman to Gypsy's left, who had been introduced as the co-ordinator of the charity, shook her head and smiled conspiratorially. 'I don't know where we'd be without him. He consistently shakes people out of their complacency and inertia. If only everyone could be as dedicated. There are far too many poseurs and charlatans standing in as concerned philanthropists.'

Gypsy swallowed painfully.

Finally he was finished—once an obscene amount of money had been bid. Everyone started to stand up and move about. Rico was coming back down to the table and, to Gypsy's surprise, with singular intent he grabbed her arm and said succinctly, 'OK I've had enough. Let's get out of here.'

Gypsy trailed after him, seeing the way

people approached him but then stood back as if intimidated by his grimness. She almost felt sorry for them. 'Don't you want to stay? Talk to people?'

He glanced back at her. 'Not unless they want to pay for my time and donate more money. Do *you* want to stay?'

Gypsy all but shuddered and shook her head eagerly. 'No.'

A questioning gleam lit his eyes for a second, but then it was gone, and he led the way until they were back in the car and driving away. Rico was already opening his bow-tie with a grimace, and the top button of his shirt. Gypsy was transfixed by his hand, those long fingers...

Suddenly his hand stopped moving, and with a panicky feeling in her gut Gypsy met speculative grey ones. He quirked a small smile. 'If you keep looking at me like that I'm going to do something about it. I meant what I said in London. I want you, and I intend to have you, Gypsy. On my bed, underneath me...'

Her face flaming now, Gypsy hissed, 'Stop that right now.'

He shrugged. 'It's going to happen, Gypsy. We might not trust each other, or even like each other very much, but that's beside the point. I won't force you, though. You'll admit you want me too before we sleep together. I'm prepared to wait…for now. But I'll warn you I'm not a patient man.'

Gypsy tried to look away but couldn't. She felt hot inside at his obvious intent, and extremely susceptible having witnessed Rico at that charity event—having seen his clear distaste for the whole scene and his obvious determination to beat the cynics at their own game.

Right now she felt very confused, because the man she'd just seen working a jaded crowd to his advantage was someone she very possibly wanted to like her. Feeling very shaky inside, she mustered up a futile and rebellious, 'Don't hold your breath…'

CHAPTER NINE

THREE days later they were sitting on Rico's plane again, winging their way back to Europe—to Greece. Rico was immersed in work at the back of the plane, and Gypsy had Lola curled sleepily on her lap, exhausted after exciting days getting to know her new cousins. She was already worshipping the ground that Beatriz walked on, and doting on Luis as if he were her own brother.

Gypsy had met Rico's mother—a small dark woman with the saddest eyes she'd ever seen. It had been clear that no familial love existed between the brothers and her, despite Isobel's valiant efforts to include her in everything. She hadn't even looked all that surprised or overjoyed at being presented with a brand-new granddaughter.

But, more than that, Gypsy couldn't get over how, in the space of the last three days, her impression of Rico had changed so much.

After witnessing his distaste at another society charity function the night after the first outing, she'd ascertained that, while he wanted to contribute something, he had as much cynicism for the monied elite as she did. Even more disconcerting had been his reaction to seeing her hair straightened again. He'd growled at her in the car. 'I don't want to see your hair like that again. In future leave it alone.'

His words had had a seismic effect on her after years of having it drummed into her by her father that she looked like an unkempt mess, not fit for polite society. Feeling more and more uncomfortable at clinging on to her prejudices, the following day Gypsy had asked Isobel if she could use the computer in the house study, and she had done what she should have done as soon as she'd found out she was pregnant. She'd run a Google search for Rico.

She'd read as much as she could, with a sinking heart and a sick feeling her belly. Far from her father's assessment of Rico—which she realised now must have come out of petty jealousy—Rico Christofides was universally lauded as one of the cleanest entrepreneurs in the world. He played harshly and ruthlessly, yes, but always fairly.

Her father's name was even mentioned in a couple of articles, citing instances when he'd tried—stupidly, by all accounts—to take over some of Rico's interests. Rico had merely swatted him back like an inconsequential fly. No wonder her father had hated him so much; he hadn't been able to beat him. And he'd been humiliated in the process.

Gypsy had even seen that while they'd been in London Rico had been involved in extremely delicate negotiations to save an electronics plant on the verge of collapse in northern England. If it had gone under it would have pushed an already economically challenged area over the edge. But Rico had managed to pull it back from the brink, and not only that but also to create more jobs in the process...

She'd felt even sicker, because those were the *negotiations* she'd taunted him about that day in the penthouse, when they'd been stuck inside thanks to the paparazzi.

She heard movement beside her, and looked over to see Rico take a seat on the other side of the cabin. Treacherous flames of desire and illicit excitement feathered through Gypsy's veins. He put his head back now and closed his eyes. Gypsy felt a lurch in her chest at seeing faint dark circles under his eyes. And when she recalled how gently he'd held Luis the day before at the christening she felt something even scarier.

Suddenly his head snapped back down. Those eyes opened and looked straight at her. Heat flooded her face when she recalled how she'd woken only that morning to find Rico on one arm, staring at her with a wicked gleam in his eye, his broad and powerful chest bare.

She'd watched, instantly awake and breathless, as he'd taken the pillow from the centre of the bed and thrown it to the other side of the room. Suddenly filled with nebulous emotions, acutely aware of how much she'd misjudged him, she'd entreated huskily, '*No*, Rico,' terrified he'd see her vulnerability.

But he'd just come closer and closed the gap between them. His skin had been hot and silky as he'd trapped her under one arm, bicep bulging. '*Yes*, Rico. I find that my patience is running very thin.'

Every nerve-point in Gypsy's body had come alive, treacherously telling of her inability to deny this desire. His head had lowered and his mouth had slanted over hers, stifling anything else she might say. After a futile moment of trying not to react to his kiss, to his proximity, Gypsy's mouth had opened and Rico had plundered ruthlessly, tongue stabbing deep, making Gypsy's back arch.

Her hands had instinctively clung to his arms, fingers digging into hard muscle. Before she'd known how he did it, the buttons of her pyjama top were undone and he was spreading the sides apart to bare her breasts to his gaze. The hardening rosy tips had tingled as he'd brushed a hand over one, and then the other.

Gypsy's breath had come fast and shallow, and when he'd lowered his head and mouth to suck one tip deep she'd all but bucked off the bed, so sensitised it had hurt.

Just as his hand had been travelling down to the waistband of her pants, a mewl had come from Lola in the other room.

They'd both stopped, waiting, and it had come again—stronger. Louder. She'd woken up. With a veritable turmoil of tangled emotions and frustrated desires in her belly Gypsy had pushed Rico away and got up, hastily buttoning her top again. Reluctantly she'd looked back to the bed, to scc Rico lying there, arms behind his head, the sheet just managing to hide the extent of his arousal, chest broad and awe inspiring, gleaming dark olive with a smattering of masculine hair.

He'd smiled wickedly and drawled, 'Next time we won't have a convenient interruption. I can promise you that…'

Gypsy had fled.

Now, as Rico's far too assessing eyes looked at her, she burned all over. She wasn't sure if it was her imagination, but she thought she'd caught him looking at her periodically over the last couple of days with a speculative gleam. He just arched a brow now, and asked laconically, 'So, did you find anything interesting on the internet?'

All the heat that had just warmed Gypsy's cheeks leached out. 'What do you mean?'

'You know exactly what I mean,' he said easily. 'Isobel told me you'd been on the internet, and it's an easy thing to check the history. I think you possibly found out everything but my shoe size.'

No wonder he'd been looking at her; he *knew* she'd been snooping. The heat flooded back— and she hadn't even found out anything about his personal life, his real father in Greece, or what had happened to him between the ages of sixteen and twenty, when he'd burst on the scene having become a dotcom millionaire overnight.

Gypsy's arms tightened across the sleeping Lola, causing her to shift slightly. Stiffly she said, 'I felt that perhaps I owed you the benefit of the doubt. I realised that I really didn't have much basis for my...' She faltered tellingly.

'*Prejudice* I think is the word you're looking for.' And then he shocked her by saying, 'Perhaps we're both guilty of the same thing. After all… you've given me very little to go on…'

Gypsy quivered inwardly at the thought of one of his many minions checking her out. 'There's nothing much to tell.'

Rico turned to face her more. 'And yet I find that's really not the case at all. You're quite the enigma. You patently didn't come after me for the easiest gold-digging opportunity in history, but the ease with which you can navigate a high-end charity event tells me you know that world. And yet you were living in a hovel when I found you.'

For the first time Gypsy felt that perhaps she could tell Rico something of her life, but then that visceral fear surged up: despite what she knew about him now, she still couldn't trust him. It held her back. There was too much at stake. He might play fair in business, but would he play fair in personal matters—especially those concerning his own daughter? He'd said he wouldn't ever forgive Gypsy for what she'd done. It was only now that she knew a little of his personal history that she could see how it might have shaped his need not to be seen rejecting his own child.

She reiterated stiffly, 'There's really nothing to tell.'

After locking eyes with her for a long moment,

until Gypsy felt breathless, Rico said, 'Why don't you take Lola and get some sleep in the bedroom? I still have work to do.'

And, as much to escape as anything else, Gypsy took his suggestion and left.

A few hours after doing some brain-numbing work which had more to do with blocking out the erotic memory of kissing Gypsy that morning, and how hard it had been to let her walk away, than any actual need to work Rico stretched and stood up.

He prowled silently to the back of the plane to look in on Gypsy and Lola, and stopped just inside the doorway with an ominous tightening in his chest. Gypsy lay on her side, her hair in a stream of curls around her head, knees up and her hand protectively on Lola's chest, cocooning her. Lola lay in complete abandon, legs and arms splayed. Gypsy had put pillows on Lola's other side to prevent her rolling off the bed.

A fierce sense of possessiveness rose up within him, and it encompassed the two people on the bed—not just the little one. The constriction in his chest not easing one bit, he walked in and pulled a blanket first of all over Gypsy, and then a smaller one over Lola. Neither one moved. He stood watching Gypsy and tried to battle the maelstrom of emotions she so effortlessly aroused.

He'd told her she was an enigma, and she was. Information on her background was starting to trickle through, and what he'd learnt so far had him reeling. He'd just given her a chance to tell him herself, but she hadn't. And he wanted to know why she was so reluctant to tell him of her past.

It was becoming harder and harder for him to cling on to his sense of injustice that she'd kept Lola secret from him. It was also becoming harder for him to remember why he didn't want to shackle her to him in marriage. The prospect, once so repugnant, now had a distinct appeal. He couldn't lie to himself that he wasn't a little envious of what Rafael and Isobel had together, and, while he didn't imagine he'd ever experience that for himself, he certainly wasn't averse to trying to create a home based around family...and mutual desire.

All Gypsy's behaviour in the past few days had pointed to her sharing a very similar moral compass to Isobel's, and he knew Isobel was not a woman who would choose to have a child and decide not to tell the father without good reason.

Gypsy's presence by his side at the social functions had been a revelation. In the past he'd had to deal with sulks and moues of disappointment from mistresses or dates when he'd wanted to do his bit and then leave as soon as possible. But he'd got the distinct impression that Gypsy had as little time for those events as he did. She'd had no desire to ogle the A-list celebrities, or talk inanities with the sycophants who all wanted a slice of him—or more accurately his fortune. In the space of two nights he'd found himself instinctively seeking her hand and relishing finding that she was right behind him without a murmur of dissent—if anything she'd shared his look of mild distaste.

And what was even more disconcerting was the ease with which he'd slipped into something that felt extremely domestic. Coming home to Lola each night, checking on her. Listening to Gypsy get up to soothe her if she woke during the night. Feeling the bed dip as she got back in and *aching* to just pull her close to him and make love to her until he could satisfy himself that what had happened between them had been a figment of his imagination.

He had a sinking feeling, as he watched her now and felt the familiar throb of desire, that it would prove to be anything but. He'd told her arrogantly that he'd wait for her to come to him, confident that she'd be mindless with desire for him, but he'd been the one to lose control that morning. Vulnerability clawed upwards again. He'd control this desire, wait until he knew more about the mother of his child. Make her *want* him as badly as he wanted her. Space. That was what he would have to impose—even if it killed him.

Lola squealed happily as Rico threw her in the air again, only to catch her in safe hands just before she touched the glittering azure water of the pool, which was half-indoors, half-outdoors. Rico had explained that this was the winter pool and was heated. Gypsy had seen another idyllic outdoor pool from the terrace where they'd had breakfast that morning.

'Again!' Lola screeched ecstatically, her favourite new word, which she'd picked up from Beatriz. Gypsy stifled a wry smile to see that Rico was fast discovering the perils of an indefatigable toddler who'd just discovered an exciting game and the power of language.

Her heart clenched to see Lola so happy in this environment—especially when she thought of their less than salubrious home in London and felt the familiar guilt. There, Lola had been lucky to get a go on the one non-mangled swing in the bleak park. Here... Gypsy sighed as she looked around from the seat she sat on. Here was paradise.

They'd landed in Athens late last night and transferred straight onto a smaller plane, which had borne them across southern Greece to the island of Zakynthos. In the surprisingly cool night air Rico had ushered them into a Jeep and had driven them himself to his villa, which was near the private airfield.

Gypsy had been too exhausted to take much notice of their surroundings last night, and had been barely aware of the friendly housekeeper Rico had introduced as Agneta. But she *had* been disturbingly aware of a new coolness from Rico. Gone were the hot and intent looks, but she was determined not to let it bother her. Rico was undoubtedly trying to unsettle her again.

This morning, when she'd carried Lola down to breakfast, she'd been in awe at the beauty of the simple yet expansive villa unfolding around her. Everything was bright and airy, with huge glass windows showcasing the fabulous views of the Mediterranean.

Agneta had met them with a wide smile and led them to where Rico was reading a paper and eating breakfast on a shaded terrace. Gypsy had been surprised, once again, that he was there and hadn't already left to go to work. She'd also been more than bemused to see a state-of-the-art highchair waiting for Lola, and she'd noticed the discreet child-proofing that had been done throughout the villa.

Rico had stood when they'd arrived, and enquired, 'I trust you slept well?'

Gypsy had just nodded and garbled, 'Yes, thank you. Our rooms are most comfortable.' Which was a huge understatement. She didn't want to admit that she'd actually missed Rico's presence in the room last night—*in the bed*. Even though she'd told herself staunchly that she'd been relieved to be shown to a suite of rooms of her own.

There was a dressing room, bathroom and sitting room. Not to mention the huge bedroom, with a four-poster bed complete with diaphanous muslin curtains drawn back. And Agneta had shown her into an equally generous ante-room which had been set up as a nursery for Lola. Gypsy had had to swallow an emotional lump, and had put it down to tiredness.

But that same lump was threatening again now, as she watched Rico and Lola frolic in the water, both sets of identical grey eyes smiling. So she knew it had nothing to do with tiredness. With each day that passed Lola was getting more and more attached to Rico. She went into his arms with no hesitation, and was already using him as someone to go to when she didn't want to do something Gypsy wanted her to do.

With that revelation making her feel uncomfortable and crabby, not to mention the far too provocative sight of a half-naked Rico, she approached the side of the pool with a towel, indicating that Lola should get out.

'She'll be impossible to put down for a nap after lunch if she gets too excited now.'

Those two sets of grey eyes turned to her, and Gypsy felt inordinately petty. But even though Rico's eyes flashed he waded to the edge of the pool and handed Lola over. Predictably, she began to protest at having her game cut short.

He drew himself out in one fluid motion which made Gypsy's breath hitch. She avoided looking at where the water sluiced off his body. She could only be thankful that he wore board shorts and not something more insubstantial.

'I should go into Athens for a few hours to tend to business. Go ahead and have dinner without me. I'll probably be late.'

Gypsy barely looked up, too afraid of what she might see. She had an awful prickling feeling that she'd *hurt* him.

As Rico sat in his car in the bumper-to-bumper traffic in central Athens his suit chafed, and he longed to rip off his tie and open his shirt. He cursed himself. He'd always loved coming back to Athens, and the anticipation of work, of seeing his mistress or the prospect of taking a new one. But that didn't appeal any more. All he could think about was the reproach in Gypsy's eyes as she'd taken Lola from him at the pool and the feeling that he'd done something wrong. And also how much he'd prefer to be there, and not here.

He cursed himself again for his weakness. The child was making him soft, and frustrated desire was clouding his brain—that was all. He cursed his vow to exercise restraint and let a new sense of anticipation fire through him as he thought of grilling his employees to see what else they'd found out about Gypsy.

By the end of their first week living at the villa Gypsy knew her nerves were wrought tight. Rico was there every morning, to greet them and have breakfast. He'd play with Lola for a while, and then disappear in a helicopter to go to Athens and work. Most evenings he'd make it back for dinner and they'd have stilted conversation—stilted because every time Rico tried to navigate into more personal waters Gypsy clammed up.

She'd heard the helicopter some time ago, and now waited with her heart thumping unevenly for Rico to appear for dinner.

When he did, striding into the room as silently

as a panther, he took her breath away—as always. He'd obviously just showered and changed. His hair was still damp, slicked back from his high forehead. The dark shirt and faded jeans made her think of that night she'd seen him in the club for the first time.

She gulped and looked away, thankful for Agneta's presence as she came in with the first course. Rico asked after Lola, and Gypsy told him that they'd taken a drive to a nearby beach and had a picnic. On their first day he'd given her the keys to a Jeep, telling her it was hers to use.

He finished his starter before her and sat back, appraising her with those unreadable silver eyes.

Gypsy felt more and more hot, wishing she'd put on something lighter than a cotton jumper and a pair of jeans. 'What is it?' she finally asked. 'Have I got something on my face?'

Rico shook his head, and then smiled, causing Gypsy to feel momentarily winded. He reached out a long arm and his fingers took a strand of her hair, letting it slip between them. His eyes met hers. 'Who made you believe you should straighten your hair?'

His touch was affecting her far too much. Gypsy pulled her head away and Rico finally let go. She pushed her unfinished starter away, her appetite gone.

Rico leant forward. 'Gypsy, either you tell me something about yourself or fifteen months of living together is going to get very tired, very quickly. And if that's your plan then give it up— because it won't work. You owe me.'

She bit her lip and played with her napkin, feeling as though she was about to walk into a chasm with no bottom in sight. 'My father... He never liked my hair left curly.' She was trembling now. She'd never spoken of her father to anyone.

'He was a fool,' Rico growled softly.

Gypsy flicked him a glance and looked away again, somehow heartened by the glint in his eye. It reminded her of an expression he had sometimes when looking at Lola. 'He used to tell me I looked like the gypsies that lived at the side of the road...so if we ever went out in public he'd insist I had it straightened.'

'Even as a child?'

Gypsy nodded.

'What about your mother? What did she think?'

Gypsy tensed perceptibly, but even Agneta coming in to take away the starters and deliver their main course didn't divert Rico's attention.

He merely repeated the question when they were alone again.

Gypsy looked at him. 'My mother got ill when I was six, and I went to live with my father.' She didn't think it worth mentioning that the least of her mother's worries at that time had been the state of Gypsy's hair.

Rico put down his fork. 'They weren't married?'

Gypsy shook her head.

'Tell me about her.'

Gypsy thought back and let a small smile play around her mouth, unaware of how Rico's gaze dropped there for a moment. 'She was Irish... and poor. Very naïve—too naïve. My father was her boss; he seduced her, and promised her all sorts of things, but when she fell pregnant he didn't want to know.'

Rico asked sharply, 'How do you know that?'

Gypsy looked at him, not really understanding the vehemence behind his question but suspecting something had hit close to his own experience. 'I guess I don't, for certain. But I know my mother kept him informed of our whereabouts and he never showed up or helped us financially. It became more obvious when she got ill and wanted him to take me in. He refused at first.' Gypsy couldn't hide the bitterness in her voice.

'He took me once he'd had a paternity test done, of course.'

She focused back on Rico and asked, 'Did something similar happen to you?'

Rico held a delicate wine glass in one hand, twirling it in long fingers. She could sense his tension.

He didn't look at her, but said, 'Something like that. My mother had an affair with a rich Greek tycoon, and when she fell pregnant he ran home. She was forced into a marriage of convenience to save her family's reputation before it became common knowledge that she was pregnant.'

He looked at her. 'Except that's not exactly how it happened.' He went on, 'I left to find my father when I was sixteen, determined to confront him for leaving us. When I eventually found him, here on Zakynthos, he had lost nearly everything and had less than a year to live. He'd always believed that my mother had had a miscarriage. He told me that he'd begged her to marry him, but that after the supposed miscarriage she'd told him to leave and never come back.'

His mouth was a grim line. 'So all those years were wasted; he thought I'd never been born, and I believed he'd not wanted to know me. And my stepfather had made my life hell because I reminded him every day of another man in my mother's bed.'

Gypsy felt emotion rising up. 'Rico...I'm so sorry. I can't imagine how bittersweet it must have been to meet your father only to lose him again.'

Rico laughed harshly. 'Don't get too romantic about it. He was a bitter old man by the time I got to him, and the best thing he did for me was leave me his ailing taverna—which I did up and sold on at a profit a few years later.' He inclined his head. 'And I changed my name, so at least I gave him that in death.'

Gypsy couldn't meet his eye; in many respects they'd trod a very similar path. She felt as if a huge lump was constricting her throat, but managed to get out, 'I can see why you were so angry to find out about Lola... I truly wouldn't have kept her from you if I'd thought I could trust you.'

'And why couldn't you trust me, Gypsy?' he asked silkily.

She looked at him. 'I still don't know that I can. From the moment you came back into my life...*our* lives...you've dominated and controlled. I grew up with someone who lived his life like that, and I know a little of what it's like to be resented for being there. I didn't want to risk putting Lola through that.'

His eyes glittered dark grey in the gathering dusk. 'It would seem as if we're at something of an impasse. You admit you can't trust me, and I'm not sure that I can forgive you for keeping me from Lola.'

Gypsy tried a wry smile, but it came out skewed. 'We only have to endure this for fifteen months and then you can get on with your life.' That damned lump was back in her throat. 'You can find someone who can match your exacting standards of moral behaviour.'

Rico reacted viscerally to the fact he'd just revealed so much about his past and to that provocative statement—even though he hated himself for reacting. He reached out to take her chin, drawing her face around to his. She wouldn't avoid him. He felt her clench her jaw against his hand, and even that had a hot spiral of desire rushing through him. 'You won't be going anywhere until we've dealt with this desire between us, Gypsy. Unfinished business, you could call it.'

Gypsy tried to pull her chin away, but couldn't. She gritted out, 'Well, let's go to bed now and get it over with, shall we?'

His eyes flared in response, and Gypsy could see something hot in their depths. Even though it caused an answering quiver in her belly, she immediately regretted her rash words. He finally let her go and sat back, draining his wine glass before saying nonchalantly, 'This will happen the way I want it, Gypsy, and it won't be to prove a point. Provoke me all you want, but you'd better be ready for the fall-out.'

Gypsy threw down her napkin and left the room.

Rico curbed the urge to drag her back and plunder her mutinous mouth. Desire was a heavy ache within him, and far too many ambiguous emotions were roiling in his chest. As for what he'd said about forgiving her—he was very much aware that forgiveness was something that had stolen over him while he wasn't even looking. He still felt regret for having missed out on Lola's early months, but no more anger towards Gypsy—and that realisation was cataclysmic.

That night Gypsy slept fitfully. She'd checked on Lola after dinner, but had been too restless to go to sleep straight away. It had seemed crazy to stay confined to her bedroom just to avoid Rico. Remembering the pool and how enticing it had looked, and the fact that it was heated, had encouraged her to think she might exercise herself to exhaustion.

It was only when she had been on the brink of walking into the pool area that she'd heard a sound and seen powerful arms scissoring in and out of the water. Mesmerised, half hidden behind a big plant, Gypsy had watched with bated breath as Rico had stopped and floated lazily on his back.

He had been completely naked. His long sleek body illuminated only by the moonlight and a few dim spotlights. Nearly tripping in her haste to get away before he saw her, Gypsy had fled back up to her room, knowing that nothing would be able to eradicate that potent image from her brain.

Now she'd woken again, and flipped onto her back, sighing heavily. She thought she'd heard a mewl come from Lola, but wasn't sure if it had been a dream or not. She got up to investigate, just in case.

At the doorway to Lola's room Gypsy felt her breath stop when her eyes registered the sight before her. Rico was asleep on a chair in the corner, his long jean-clad legs spread out before him, wearing a worn T-shirt which he must have pulled on after his swim. Powerful arms cradled the sleeping form of Lola to his chest.

Lola's legs were curled up and her thumb was in her mouth, her other hand curled trustingly on Rico's chest. For a second Gypsy feared she might cry out, so intense was the emotion ripping through her.

Controlling herself with an effort, she could

see that though Rico might be asleep he must be uncomfortable. On bare feet she padded over and, bending down, barely breathing, carefully started to put her hands underneath Lola to lift her up.

Immediately Rico's hands tensed in an instinctively protective gesture, and his eyes snapped open. Silently Gypsy communicated with him, and willed down the response of her body to his proximity, suddenly very aware of her short nightdress.

Relaxing his hold, Rico let Gypsy lift Lola away. Her legs went weak as her hands felt the hard contours of Rico's chest. Carefully she stepped back and placed Lola down into the cot, pulling a blanket over her, and prayed that Rico would be gone when she turned around.

But he wasn't. He was sitting forward, elbows on his knees, looking at her with slumberous eyes. One lock of midnight-black hair had fallen over his forehead. Hot all over, Gypsy backed away to her bedroom and watched with widening eyes as Rico stood up and prowled towards her.

Taking her by the hand, he put a finger to her mouth before she could say anything and looked at Lola. Gypsy nodded and let him lead her out. Her heart palpitated at the thought that he'd come through her bedroom to get to Lola, having obviously heard the same cry she'd heard earlier.

Expecting him to let her go now they were out of Lola's room, with the door pulled behind them, Gypsy tried to pull her hand away—but Rico wouldn't let go. She looked up, and all she could see were two burning pools of stormy grey.

She knew that look. She *ached* for that look. She'd seen that look in dreams for two years. But even so she shook her head. The need to protect herself against this final capitulation was strong. She opened her mouth to speak, but Rico put his finger there again and came close, backing her against the wall and pressing close, so close that Gypsy couldn't think. All she could see was that image of him naked in the pool. Heat exploded low in her belly.

His voice was low and sultry. 'This is inevitable—as inevitable as it was that night two years ago. We've both been waiting for this... wanting this...'

Gypsy shook her head again, futilely, and Rico speared his hands through her hair either side of her face, his thumbs on her jaw.

'You're mine, Gypsy, and there will be no more waiting. Your body tells me what you refuse to.'

And he bent his head and kissed her

passionately, tipping her head back so that he could stab deep with his tongue. Desire was instant and overwhelming. Gypsy didn't have a hope. She was a bundle of vulnerabilities, and at every turn this man was only making her feel more vulnerable, giving her little to cling onto in the way of protection.

Feeling impotent, and angry at her weakness, Gypsy fought fire with fire. Stroking Rico's tongue with hers, she exulted in his hitched breath as he recognised her capitulation.

Gypsy's hands came to his T-shirt and snaked underneath. She needed to feel his chest. Moving her hands over him, she felt how his belly contracted when she scraped her nails over the smooth skin and moved higher, through the covering of hair, finding the blunt nipples.

Impatient to see him, she pulled at the T-shirt. He ripped it off completely. He bent down for a second, and Gypsy felt herself being lifted into his arms and carried to the bed before Rico put her down again, sliding her down his body so that her nightdress rode up over her thighs.

She tried to move back, but with his hands on her waist he wouldn't let her budge. His eyes were burning down into hers. She couldn't look away, and felt heat flood her cheeks when he rocked his hips against her and she could feel the thrust of his erection against his jeans and her belly.

Liquid heat seeped between her legs and Gypsy squirmed. Breathless, she reached up and wound her arms around his neck, searching for and finding his mouth, savouring the firm fullness of his lower lip. His big hands moved to her bottom, underneath her pants, which he pushed down as he caressed her, coming back up over the indent of her waist and pulling her nightdress upwards.

For a split second Gypsy hesitated, her pants around her thighs and her nightdress bunched up just under her breasts. And then, with a deep shaky breath, she lifted her arms and let Rico pull it up and off all the way. Dimly, she knew he would not deviate from his mission. And the clamour in her own pulse told her that, no matter what she might protest, she was as hungry for this as he was.

She felt her hair fall down over her shoulders, and watched as Rico reached out to twine the strands around his hand. She brought up her hands to cover her breasts and he smiled down at her wolfishly. 'It's a bit late for modesty, don't you think?'

Gypsy bit her lip. Rico bent down and pressed a kiss to her shoulder. Shuddering, she let her head fall back, and she felt his hands come to her pants, pushing them down her legs completely.

She was barely aware of him taking something out of his jeans pocket before she heard the button snap and the zip come down. They were gone, and he stood before her naked and proud.

Unable to stop herself, she let her gaze drop almost greedily. A part of her balked at his size, despite having been with him before, but another part *thrilled*.

Hoarsely Rico said, 'Touch me, Gypsy… please…'

She reached out and closed one hand around his length, feeling a shudder go through his big frame. She'd touched him like this on that first night too. He moved closer, put his hand to the back of her head, and while she kept her hand on him, moving up and down, he tipped her face up to his and kissed her.

He trailed his other hand down her body, caressing the side of one breast, its full outline, causing her own hand to stop momentarily. Then he continued down over her waist and her belly.

Mouths fused, Gypsy groaned deeply when she felt his hand seek between her legs, pushing them apart, stroking through her curls to where she burned wetly for him. Her hand stopped moving on him again for a moment when she felt the slide of his fingers along her wetness, slipping inside.

Her body clenched in an automatic reaction.

He tore his mouth away and said harshly, '*Dio*. How could I have forgotten how responsive you are…?'

Gypsy made a soft mewl. She ached all over. Her breasts throbbed, their peaks so tight and hard they almost hurt.

As if sensing her building agitation, Rico took her hand from him and pushed her back onto the bed. 'Gypsy, I don't know if I can go slowly…'

She lifted her head, feeling all at once slumberous and wide awake. Half incoherent with lust, she replied, 'I don't want slow.'

She vaguely heard the ripping of a packet before he was back between her legs, hairroughened chest crushing her breasts. Blindly she drew up her legs and reached for his buttocks, her hands feathering along his hips.

He put one arm under her back, arching her up to him, and as he thrust into her he bent and sucked one nipple deep. Gypsy had to bite her hand to stop crying out loud.

With his steady thrusts, past and present mingled into one moment for Gypsy. She'd always thought she'd imbued their night together with something *more* than it was. That it couldn't possibly have been as earth-shattering as she remembered.

But what was happening now *was* even more than she remembered. Little fires danced all over her skin. Sweat dewed her body. She burned and ached at the same time for the elusive pinnacle. Her hips moved in tandem with Rico's. He was a master of torture, bringing them close, only to pull back again. Constantly hovering near the edge.

Close to emotional tears that she didn't have the strength to hide, Gypsy husked, 'Rico, please…'

And finally, unleashing his full awe-inspiring power, Rico gave in to the devil inside him and drove Gypsy over the shattering edge before letting himself fall behind her.

After a brief respite, it was Gypsy who turned to Rico and started to press tiny kisses all down his chest and hard belly. He tensed as she found that rapidly recovering part of him and took him into her mouth.

Sucking in a breath of pure arousal, struggling to retain control, he reached down to pull her away before she made him explode completely. Drawing her up so that she straddled him, he shifted her with big hands on her hips so that her hot, wet core slid down on him, encircling him in that tight heat.

With his legs bent, Rico clenched his jaw not to come just at the sight of Gypsy finding her rhythm, sliding up and down his shaft, which felt fuller and harder than he could ever remember. His hands cupped her breasts, thumbs flicking her nipples, before he came up to take one and then the other into his mouth.

In some dim recess of his mind, as her movements became more frantic, as she pushed him back and bent down over his chest to press a kiss to his mouth, her hard nipples scraping against his chest, Rico knew that any hope he'd had that their night together hadn't been as stupendous as in his memory was blown to smithereens. Because it had just been eclipsed.

CHAPTER TEN

'I KNOW when you're awake, Gypsy. You go very still and your breathing changes. I was aware of it every moment you lay pretending to sleep in Buenos Aires.'

Gypsy opened her eyes and met Rico's grey ones. Her heart thudded painfully and her cheeks flooded with colour. She couldn't bear to think of how wanton she'd been last night. Or how easily she'd capitulated.

He was propped up on one elbow. The curtains were open and she saw that he was clean-shaven and wearing a white shirt and jeans. Panic gripped her, and she would have thrown back the cover but remembered that she was naked.

'What time is it? Where's Lola?'

'She's dressed and downstairs, with Agneta and her grandson. He's the same age.'

Gypsy looked at him suspiciously. 'You changed her nappy?'

Rico grimaced. 'Yes, after a few attempts.'

Something in Gypsy's insides melted but she fought it. 'I should get up.'

Rico leaned back and put his hands behind his head. 'Go ahead. I'm not stopping you.'

Gypsy bit out, 'I'm naked.'

He said with a mock-lascivious leer, 'I know.' And then more seriously, when she didn't move, 'Are you telling me that after last night you feel modest?'

Gypsy all but groaned, and went even redder. Her hands clenched on the sheet and she looked around desperately for something to cover up. Taking pity on her, Rico got off the bed and went to the bathroom, coming back with a robe. He wouldn't turn around, though, and watched mockingly as Gypsy contorted herself to get into the robe without revealing anything of her body.

Her body upon which she could already see the marks of having been made love to. Eventually she stood up, but gasped when Rico grabbed the lapels of the robe and pulled her into him.

She looked up, her belly spasming treacherously. 'Rico, we can't—not here, now…'

'As much as I'm looking forward to making love to you again, Gypsy, I won't right now. What I am going to say is this: I don't want to hear one word of regret or recrimination. You'll be moved into my rooms as of today, and Lola will be set up in the suite adjoining mine.'

Gypsy went to speak, but Rico cut off whatever she was about to say when his mouth slanted over hers and he took advantage of her open mouth. Within seconds the flames of passion rose around them, and before Gypsy knew it Rico had stopped kissing her and she was clinging helplessly to his T-shirt. She saw the burning intent in his eyes and it made her tremble in response. How could she deny that she wanted this too, after last night? She'd be the worst kind of liar.

Amidst the desire heating her blood trickled something cold, though—Rico was just controlling her, dominating her exactly as he'd been doing all along. It made her say now, as she stepped back and willed her legs to hold her up, 'I won't say anything about regret or recrimination, but I want to keep my own room. We have a baby monitor. If I go to you we can still hear if Lola wakes up.'

Rico trailed one finger down over her flushed cheek and spoke musingly. 'Still so sure that you have something to be afraid of?'

Gypsy bit back the words trembling on her lips. She *did* have something to be *very* afraid of—and it had to do with the fact that the thought of inviting such intimacy with Rico was terrifying to her equilibrium. What was left of it.

Rico said now, 'Fine—have it your way. As long as you're in my bed every night…or I'm in yours…the geographics aren't important.'

And over the next two weeks Rico proved that Gypsy's independent stance was really just a mockery. If he went to her bed he didn't leave till the morning, and then usually only to stroll provocatively naked across the hall to his own room. And if she woke in his bed he wouldn't let her leave easily. So invariably all they were doing was using their own rooms to change and wash.

Even more disturbing, when she saw Rico return from work in the evenings on the days he went to Athens, she was aware of a spreading warmth she couldn't dampen down, no matter how much she tried.

It emanated right from her heart outwards, and it encompassed Rico now, as he strolled out to the terrace where she played with Lola as the sun set over the sea in the background.

'*Kalispera, mi pequeña,*' he said, before plucking Lola up and planting a kiss to both cheeks, which had her giggling delightedly.

'You'll confuse her with two different

languages,' Gypsy mock-scolded, slightly breathless at the way her body responded to the hot look Rico gave her. In that moment a part of her yearned for him to come and kiss her too, and she hated that she did. Wanting that kind of intimate display of affection was dangerous, because it meant she wanted more.

'Nonsense,' Rico dismissed arrogantly. 'She's my daughter therefore she is of above average intelligence and will be bilingual by the time she's three.'

Gypsy's heart thumped so hard for a moment that she put her hand up to her chest, afraid Rico might hear it. This easy banter made her feel weak with longing. Forcing herself to push down the treacherous and confusing desires of her heart, she got up abruptly, brushing grit off her jeans.

With Lola still in his arms, happily trying to pull his tie apart with chubby hands, Rico said, 'There's a function in Athens tomorrow night. I'd like you to accompany me.'

Gypsy stifled a grimace. 'A charity event?'

Rico smiled. 'No, it's a party to celebrate the opening of a friend's new hotel.'

'Oh…' Gypsy faltered. What could she say? She couldn't hide here on the island for ever, but the thought of going out in public with Rico when her feelings for him were see-sawing all over the place was very dangerous. But of course she couldn't explain that—and he'd wonder what was wrong if she gave an excuse. She shrugged, 'OK...'

'Good. I'll have Demi come pick you up around four and bring you over in the helicopter. I'll meet you at the hotel.'

Still breathless, Gypsy followed Rico as he strode back into the villa with Lola. 'Wait—what about Lola?'

He halted and turned back. 'Agneta will be here. She can watch her overnight.'

Gypsy gasped. 'We'll be gone all night? But I've never left her alone for a night.'

That familiar implacability came back into the lines of Rico's face. 'Which is why it seems to me that it's a good idea to start now. I get invited to things all the time, and it's more practical to stay in Athens. We could bring her with us if we had a nanny, but as we don't...'

Gypsy felt the wrench of being parted from Lola already. 'We don't need a nanny. I can take care of her—'

'Not all the time.' Rico's tone brooked no argument, and he turned to stride inside again, throwing back over his shoulder, 'Now that you've brought it up, I'll arrange to have some nannies sent to the villa for interview in the next few days.'

'You're doing it again.' Gypsy almost had to run after Rico, watching as he handed Lola over to Agneta, who indicated that she would feed her. When Agneta had left with Lola, Rico turned to her with a dangerous look on his face.

'I am a busy man. Part of this fifteen-month deal is that you are by my side as my companion. We can't do that with a baby. She will be fine. Rafael and Isobel have a nanny for exactly that purpose.'

'That's Rafael and Isobel,' Gypsy said, afraid he'd hear the bitterness in her voice. 'They're different.'

He came close then, and Gypsy backed away, suddenly intimidated by the dangerous light in his eyes. 'Why? Because they're a real couple?'

'Something like that,' Gypsy flung at him, hoping he'd stop coming towards her. But he didn't.

'There's no reason we can't be that, Gypsy… we have desire…'

Gypsy spluttered, shocked to feel a rush of something that felt disturbingly like *hope*. 'That agreement you mentioned is *your* agreement. If you can recall, I didn't have much say in it. And Rafael and Isobel have a lot more than desire. You don't even *like* me!'

Rico stopped, a muscle in his jaw pulsing. 'I think it's safe to say that what I feel for you is undergoing something of a metamorphosis. And, to be perfectly honest, fifteen months is looking less and less palatable. I envisage a much longer union. It's practical on every level...especially when I don't see any sign of our desire waning...'

Feeling sheer panic at his cold words, and wanting to know what he'd meant by saying his feelings were changing, let alone the prospect that he'd want to lock her into some sort of loveless but passionate union, she blurted out, 'Well, I can't guarantee that my desire will last much longer. And I'm sure your ego won't relish taking to bed a woman who doesn't desire you any more. So perhaps you should think of that before you make any rash pronouncements.'

The words were stupid—inspired by panic and completely untrue, much to her own dismay. If anyone was going to lose their desire she had no doubt it would be Rico. She saw his expression change and knew she had to run—fast. She did turn, as if to flee, but Rico caught her easily with his arms around her waist. Gypsy struggled against the inevitable way her body was already responding and half kicked out fruitlessly as Rico carried her into his nearby study, shutting the door behind him.

Her back was against the door and Rico was crowding her, saying dangerously, 'You were saying?'

Gypsy couldn't open her mouth. As Rico spoke his fingers made quick work of opening the buttons of her shirt. His hips ground into hers, and with his hands he pushed apart the shirt, baring her lace-covered breasts to his gaze.

Her breasts heaved with the effort it took just to stay standing, and even though on some level Gypsy was aghast at her instant response she couldn't help it. She could feel her nipples harden and push against the lace of her bra, and Rico saw it too, a feral smile curling his lips as he cupped her breasts and brushed his thumbpads over the straining peaks. Gypsy bit back a moan.

'I don't see any evidence of your desire waning. *This* does not happen to everyone…' Rico's voice was guttural. 'It's been instantaneous between us since we met. Do you think it'll burn out when a two-year absence couldn't dampen it?'

Gypsy fought through the waves of desire threatening to suck her under and said defiantly, 'Nothing lasts for ever.'

With anger and desire crackling between them, Rico took Gypsy's mouth in a bruising kiss. Her treacherous hands acted independently of her will and went to his tie to pull it off. Frantically she opened the buttons on his shirt, hearing some pop and fall to the ground. While her hands were on his belt he pushed down the lace cups of her bra, freeing her breasts to his mouth, where he sucked and nipped gently at the sensitised peaks.

Gypsy pushed down his trousers and freed his heavy erection. Rico flicked open her jeans and pushed them down, along with her panties.

'Kick them off and put your legs around my waist.'

Gypsy nearly wept with frustration when her jeans got stuck, bending down to pull them off before reaching up again to cling onto Rico's neck and shoulders as he took her legs and wrapped them around him. They hadn't even moved from the door.

With one smooth and powerful thrust he embedded himself within her. Gypsy gasped out loud, clutching him tightly as he slowly withdrew and then thrust in again. He loosened her hold and set her back against the door, putting some space between them so that he could bend his head and take one rosy-tipped breast into his mouth as he thrust rhythmically.

When he took his mouth away from her breast Gypsy opened her eyes and looked at him. His cheeks were slashed with colour, his face stark with need and passion, his eyes nearly black. With a welling of emotion she acted completely instinctively and clasped his face in her hands, bringing his mouth to hers.

As they approached their shattering crescendo their mouths clung, and Rico swallowed her loud moan as she clenched around him more powerfully than he'd felt before. Then he let himself go, and spilled his life seed into her with such an intensity of feeling that when it was over he could only bury his head in her neck and try to remember which way was up.

They stayed like that for a long moment, the air cooling their hot skin, still intimately joined, and Gypsy stroked Rico's hair, not even aware of the tenderness of her gesture.

In that moment when Rico felt Gypsy's hand in his hair, something fundamental within him changed for ever. He might have just impregnated her. And, if truth be told, he hoped he had. Reeling with that knowledge, he couldn't deny it any more. He had to face up to the fact that his feelings for Gypsy had changed utterly.

Resolve gave him the strength to move, and he carefully let her down, holding her when her legs weren't steady. He could feel the tremors still running through her body. He handed her her clothes, before picking up his own and putting them on. Never in his life had such intense urgency dictated his actions. He winced inwardly. 'Are you all right?'

Gypsy looked up from where she'd just pulled her jeans up. She looked dazed. 'I…think so.'

Rico frowned, fear tightening his insides. 'Did I hurt you?'

Gypsy blushed and shook her head, her hair falling forward to hide her expression from him. 'No…you didn't hurt me.'

With that sense of resolve running through him and gathering force, Rico tipped up her chin. Her cheeks were flushed, lips swollen from his kisses, eyes huge. He had to curb the resurgence of desire. 'If you think our desire is on the wane, or that this is something that happens more than once in a lifetime, then you're a more cynical person than I thought you were.'

Gypsy looked at Rico, her heart pounding all over again. He was looking back at her with an indecipherable expression on his face.

'But…you're not a once-in-a-lifetime person.'

His mouth tightened. 'You don't know what I am, Gypsy, because since the morning after we met and you found out who I was you've had me sized up and boxed away.'

Gypsy felt little flutters enter her belly, along with a panicky feeling. 'I don't know what you're saying, Rico.'

'What I'm saying is that you have to open up to me, Gypsy. You need to trust me. I'm not letting you go, but I'm not going to put up with your blinkered view for ever. I am in your life and in Lola's life for the foreseeable future. For that to work we need to agree on things like a nanny, and you need to be by my side when I need you.'

Inwardly shaking at his assertion that she needed to trust him and feeling extremely exposed to think that he'd made love to her just to make a point, Gypsy blurted out, 'Just like I need to be available for a quickie when the mood takes you?'

Rico's thumb moved back and forth over Gypsy's skin. All he said was, 'We both wanted what just happened. Don't pretend you didn't. And, just as I've never before picked up a woman in a club for a night of anonymous sex, I've also never felt that same urgency we felt just now. You have a unique effect on me, Gypsy Butler.'

Just then they heard Lola's chatter. Agneta had obviously finished feeding her and was looking for them. Feeling very flushed and disheveled, Gypsy pushed past Rico to open the study door, and tried to pretend that everything was normal when the world felt anything but.

At the door she turned and said to Rico, while

avoiding his eye, 'I'm quite tired tonight. I'm going to go to bed early. *Alone.*'

Rico said with a mocking drawl, 'Don't worry, Gypsy. I won't come to your bed this evening. I'll be gone early in the morning, but be ready to come to me in Athens at four o'clock tomorrow.'

That night, sleepless in bed, *aching* for Rico despite her words, Gypsy lay and stared at the ceiling in the dark. She needed to think but her mind was disturbingly fuzzy. She'd got the distinct impression from Rico's comments earlier that he saw some sort of future for them. But what, exactly? And was she brave enough to ask him?

She turned over on her side and looked out of the window to where the sea was just a black mass, with the small lights of boats flickering on and off. Rico was right. She'd prejudged him and misjudged him every step of the way.

He was nothing like her father in the business sense. And she now knew from his own personal history why he'd been so adamant that he wanted Lola. But still, that didn't account for the way he'd so instinctively taken to fatherhood. He was nothing like her father in that regard either.

Shamefully, she had to acknowledge that part of her reaction could have come from jealousy at seeing how unreservedly Rico had accepted Lola. She'd never received that from her own father. She could also see that a lot of his initial arrogance had most likely been due to shock, and perhaps a fear that she might try to run away again. He'd done everything he could to make sure they didn't leave his side.

But more than all of that was the way she felt about him. She couldn't help but remember the way he'd been that night they'd met for the first time. The magic that had infused the air as the dark and handsomely seductive stranger had put her at ease, made her laugh, and then made love to her with an intensity that had left her in pieces. Knowing Rico as she did now, she suspected that he'd indulged in a much lighter, less cynical version of himself that night. Perhaps because he had been unburdened by his anonymity, just as she had been.

If she was truly honest with herself, amidst all the turmoil of her pregnancy and finding out who Rico was, the one thing that had superceded everything else had been the hurt that he'd left her so coldly. And yet he'd admitted that he'd regretted it, that he'd tried to get in touch with her.

Gypsy's heart squeezed. She didn't think she could ever hope that Rico would look at her with the tenderness she'd seen between Rafael and Isobel, but right now her silly heart couldn't help longing for it. She couldn't fool herself into thinking that whatever rapprochement was between them would absolve her of her actions in his eyes.

The crows of doubt mocked her for even *thinking* that she might be falling for him. It had only been a few weeks since she'd met Rico again—how could she trust her feelings when her daughter's future happiness was at risk? Who was to say that Rico wasn't just seducing her to keep her and Lola in his complete control, only for him to lose interest and move on, having torn their lives apart?

The old fear was still strong, making her feel as if she should be suspicious of the way he was bonding with Lola. She hated it, but it squeezed like a vice around her heart; it was ingrained within her after years of living with a man who had bullied and controlled her because he'd resented her, the reminder of his weakness. A man who had thought nothing of letting her mother die because she was socially undesirable, and because she'd forced his hand so that he'd had to acknowledge his daughter.

Thoughts and memories roiled sickeningly in Gypsy's head until she finally fell into a dreamless sleep.

Gypsy looked at herself in the mirror of the wardrobe in a luxurious suite at the brand-new hotel that was opening that evening. A car had met her from the helicopter at the airport and whisked her here to the hotel, where she'd been met by a veritable entourage.

Up in the suite there had been a wardrobe of different outfits, and once she'd picked one out the team had set to work. The hairdresser had even smiled and said to her, 'I'm under the strictest instructions not to straighten your hair.' Gypsy had just smiled back weakly, feeling a plummeting sensation in her belly—as if she were falling over an edge into a dark chasm of the unknown.

Now she was on her own again, and twisting and turning to see herself, feeling all at once ridiculous and disturbingly *sexy*. The dress was a dark gold colour, fitted and to the knee, with just one wide strap over one shoulder, leaving the other bare.

High-heeled gold sandals looked like the most delicate things she'd ever seen and her hair was down, with Grecian-style gold bands holding it back from her face. She wore simple gold hoop earrings.

It was only then that she noticed the tall, dark and looming shape lounging against the door behind her. She whirled around, feeling very exposed. Rico was stunning in a black suit, white shirt, black tie. He straightened up and strolled towards her, and she could see that he was holding a champagne bottle and two glasses. Immediately her stomach roiled at the sight, but she clamped down on it; surely now she could take the opportunity to get over that awful teenage trauma?

Rico stared at her as if he'd never seen her before, raking his eyes up and down her body, and then he said simply, 'You look beautiful.'

Gypsy grimaced and wanted to squirm.

Rico smiled. 'Say, *Thank you, Rico.*'

She looked at him and felt an alien lightness bubble up. She smiled too. 'Thank you, Rico. You look lovely too.'

He poured champagne into two flutes and handed her one. Gypsy instinctively held her breath as she took a sip. It slid down her throat like an effervescent sunburst and she almost shouted with relief. She'd gone clammy for a moment, expecting to feel the old urge to be sick. But it hadn't come. She took another sip, relishing it.

Rico touched his glass to hers and said, 'You look like you've never tasted champagne before.'

Gypsy caught his eyes. 'Not for a long time.'

He arched a brow and asked, 'Secrets of a hell-raising youth?'

Gypsy hid the dart of pain and said, 'Hardly.'

A delicious coil of tension settled in her belly as she took Rico in; he was so tall and broad. His face all planes and shadows and hollows.

On an impulse, she blurted out, 'What happened to your nose?'

Rico stiffened. She could see his hand tighten on his glass, but then he said, 'My stepfather, the day I left Buenos Aires… He left me with a token of his affection, and a constant reminder that your own flesh and blood is your only real family.'

Gypsy remembered Isobel telling her how Rico had nearly had to be hospitalised.

'Was he responsible for the scars on your back too?' She'd noticed the faint silvery lines crisscrossing his back one morning when Rico had got up to go back to his own room, and she'd felt them while making love, but she hadn't had the nerve to ask about them. Until now.

Rico's mouth was a thin line. 'Yes, more of

my stepfather's legacy for not being his biological son. It's hard to get out of the way of a belt when you're small…'

Sheer horror tightened her gut, and she had a sudden stark understanding of how important it was for him to be there for Lola.

Gypsy went close and reached up her hand to touch his jaw. Her voice was husky. 'If I'd been there I would have stepped in the way, so he'd hit me instead.'

She looked up at him. A part of her couldn't believe what she'd just said, and another part felt fiercely that she'd meant every word. Even now anger bubbled low to think of anyone beating Rico, or hurting him.

Realisation hit her like a thunderbolt. *God*, she'd fallen for him. There was no luxury of *falling* about it. She was already deeply and profoundly in love with this man.

To her relief, before Rico might see something of her realisation and her reaction, he took the champagne and put it down before taking her hand.

His voice sounded rough, and impacted upon her somewhere very raw. 'We should go downstairs. The grand opening will be any minute now, and I have a speech to make.'

Feeling as though the earth had shifted on its

axis, Gypsy followed Rico out, her hand tightly clasped in his. All the way down in the lift she looked resolutely at the floor, terrified that if she looked into his eyes he'd know immediately.

Rico stared at the elevator door on the way down, Gypsy's hand in his. He was still reeling from her simple assertion that if she'd been there she would have taken the blows for him. He knew she'd been sincere because she'd looked shocked once the words were out—as if she couldn't believe she'd said them.

The only other person who knew the extent of what Rico had been through at the hands of his stepfather was Rafael, because he'd suffered too—albeit not to the same extent—and many times Rico had felt that Rafael wanted to say something similar. That if he could have borne the brunt of that man's anger he would have. But he'd never articulated it the way Gypsy just had, with such sweet simplicity.

Taking a deep breath just before the doors opened, Rico gripped Gypsy's hand more tightly momentarily, and she squeezed him back in silent communication. His chest expanded, the door opened, and they stepped out and into the melee.

Rico had made his speech and was now back at Gypsy's side, holding her hand again.

A guilty part of her revelled in this newly proprietorial touch and she grimaced inwardly. She could never have imagined *this*—wanting to be claimed so publicly by him.

They barely needed to circulate, as a constant stream of people came to *him*. The only time he crossed the room it was to another couple, and Rico slapped the man on his back playfully. He introduced the handsome man and his very pregnant wife to Gypsy. 'I'd like you to meet some newlywed friends of mine—Leo Parnassus and his wife Angel.'

The wife smiled shyly, one hand on her large bump. Gypsy asked how far along she was, and they started to chat about pregnancy and birth. She could feel Rico tense by her side, and when the couple had moved on he turned to her and said, 'I don't know anything about your pregnancy, or the birth...'

Guilt rose up, so much more poignant now, and immediately fearing some kind of reprisal Gypsy took her hand from his. 'I'm sorry... I didn't think...' she started.

But Rico took her hand again and shook his head. 'No, it's not about that. I'm not angry about that...not any more. But I'd like you to tell me some time, OK?'

Gypsy nodded, feeling herself fall even further into the chasm. But just at that moment,

with absolutely no sense of foreboding whatsoever, she heard someone near them declare
shrilly, 'Oh, my *God*! Alexandra Bastion, is that
you?'

CHAPTER ELEVEN

GYPSY's blood went cold. Unbeknownst to her, her hand had tightened painfully on Rico's. The woman came over and grabbed Gypsy's arm. Gypsy recognised her through the fog of shock. They'd gone to school together—a remote and very exclusive boarding school in the Outer Hebrides in Scotland. The furthest place her father had been able to find to send her.

'Alexandra—I don't believe it! It's been—what?—seven years sincc we left that place? How *are* you? What have you been up to?'

The woman's eyes went appreciatively to Rico. Clearly she was looking for an introduction. But Gypsy was incapable of speaking, and suddenly, on top of this shock, she knew the taste of the champagne was making itself felt and that she was going to be sick.

As if realising her turmoil, and no doubt thinking the woman was mad, Rico put his arm around Gypsy's waist and said urbanely, 'I'm sorry—you must have the wrong person.' With a smooth move he glided them away.

Gypsy got out through numb lips, 'I need a bathroom.'

She could hear the woman behind them saying to someone, 'How strange. I could have sworn that was Alexandra Bastion…and *who* was that guy?'

Her voice faded away, but Gypsy felt clammy all over and knew that if Rico hadn't been holding onto her she might have fallen.

In seconds they were in the lift and going upwards, a wall of tense silence between them. Gypsy took deep breaths and concentrated on not being sick, but all she could think of was the champagne sloshing around her belly, and she knew it had been that woman who had sent her back in time.

As soon as they were in the suite she ran for the bathroom and closed the door, hunching over the toilet bowl as the contents of her belly came up. She was aware of the door opening and Rico coming in. She put out a hand and said weakly, 'No, please…go away.'

But, predictably, he ignored her. She heard water running, and then she felt a damp cloth against her face and it was wonderful. Eventually, when her stomach was empty, Rico helped her up and handed her a toothbrush with toothpaste already on it. She brushed her teeth and splashed water on her face. And then Rico lifted her into his arms, despite her weak protest, and took her over to one of the ornately covered chairs and sat her down.

He went and sat on the corner of the bed, near the chair, and just watched her, hands linked loosely between his legs. Gypsy knew without him saying a word that she had to talk. *Now.* With a tight knot in her belly, she took a deep breath.

'When I was fifteen years old my father found me tasting champagne from a leftover bottle after one of his parties.' Her belly tightened at the memory. 'He dragged me into his study, opened a new bottle of champagne and forced me to drink the lot. He wouldn't let me leave the room until I had. When I was sick all over the floor he made me clean it up, and told me that perhaps I'd remember that lesson if I ever wanted to taste champagne again.'

She looked at Rico. His eyes bored into hers and he said, 'Your father was John Bastion.'

Gypsy couldn't even feel surprised that he knew. She just nodded wearily. 'When did you find out?'

'Before we came back to Athens.'

So he'd known for the past few weeks, but said nothing.

He saw the question in her eyes and said, 'I wanted you to tell me yourself. Why didn't you want to tell me about him?'

Her heart clenched. She bit her lip. Where to start? Hands closed tight in her lap, she finally said, 'Because I hated him, and from the day he died I wanted to forget that he'd existed.'

Rico frowned. 'Where did *Alexandra* come from?'

'He didn't want me. The only reason he took me in eventually was because he was a so-called pillar of society and Social Services couldn't understand why he wouldn't. He had to; he wanted to avoid negative press attention at all costs. But the minute I was under his roof he insisted on changing my name to Alexandra, and he spread the word discreetly that he'd adopted me out of the goodness of his heart. He didn't want anyone to know I was his biological daughter. He was ashamed to be reminded that he'd had an affair with a cleaner. He was ashamed of everything about me—especially as I wasn't some sleek blonde, like his own mother or his new wife.'

Rico stood up and started to pace. He turned around. 'And what about your mother? Where was she?'

Gypsy's hands tightened. She looked down. 'We weren't well off at all… Where I was living with Lola was a palace compared to where we were. She couldn't cope. She tried to kill herself...that's why she wanted me to go to my father. He insisted they send her to a mental hospital for psychiatric assessment...and without any resources or anyone to speak for her she got lost in the system, forgotten about. She died there when I was about thirteen, but I didn't find out until after my father died and I found a letter from the hospital.' She didn't mention the heartbreaking letters from her mother.

'Your father and stepmother died in a plane crash?'

Gypsy looked up again and nodded. 'Over the English Channel, coming back from France.'

Surprising her, he asked, 'Why were you in the club that night, Gypsy?'

Feeling the quiver of trepidation in her belly, but knowing that if he investigated further he'd find out everything anyway, she told him. She smiled wryly, but it felt a bit skewed. 'As I was officially my father's next of kin, despite public perception, I received everything in his will. He'd never got around to making sure I wouldn't, which is undoubtedly what he'd planned, but as he believed he was infallible he hadn't counted on sudden death...

'That night...the night of the club...it was six months after his death and I'd just received and signed over every single Bastion asset and property to all the charities he had been patron of and had stolen from for years. I felt so guilty that I'd never been brave enough to report him to the police it was the least I could do. I donated the rest of his money to psychiatric care and research. I insisted it was done anonymously. I didn't want any media attention. And I'd also just reverted back to my own birth name, which was easy as it was on my birth certificate. I was finally free—from him and his legacy. I didn't want a penny of his money. Not after what he did to my mother and how he treated me.'

She shrugged. 'I heard the beat of the music and I wanted to dance, to celebrate being free…'

Rico came and sat back down heavily on the bed.

Gypsy continued with a rush, wanting to make Rico understand. 'He knew that I knew about his transgressions with charity funds, so when I was seventeen he took me to a charity event and auctioned me off to work for a summer with that charity's operation in Africa.' Her mouth twisted. 'It was to get me out of his hair, but also a punishment and a way to demonstrate his control. I had the last laugh, though, because it was the best experience I ever had and it inspired me to want to study psychology.'

She bit her lip. 'He spoke of you. He was

envious of your fortune and said you were ruth-less. That was another reason I believed the worst about you. I assumed your methods were the same as his...'

Rico's lip curled. 'I never had anything to do with the man. I had no respect for the way he did business.'

Feeling unaccountably sad, Gypsy said, 'I know that now.' She stood up abruptly. Emotions were bubbling too close to the surface. She'd never revealed this much to another living soul and she suddenly felt too exposed. 'Look, do you mind if we don't talk about it anymore? It's in the past now. Alexandra Bastion never really existed. I'd like to go home to Lola tonight, if it's possible.'

Rico stood too, tall and powerful, his face and eyes unreadable. Gypsy nearly sagged with relief when he said, 'Of course it's possible. I'll call Demi now. Why don't you get changed and we'll go?'

The whole way back to the island, and then to the villa, Rico was silent, and Gypsy was grate-ful. Once they got inside, though, and they'd both looked in on Lola, who slept peacefully, Rico trailed a finger down Gypsy's cheek and said, 'We'll talk in the morning...we need to talk about this.'

His steely tone brooked no argument. Of

course he wasn't going to let her revelations end here. Reluctantly Gypsy nodded briefly, and Rico stepped away and strode from her room, leaving her alone.

And that night, for the first time in a long time, she slept like a baby.

The following morning Gypsy revelled in waking up to Lola's chatter as she waited contentedly for someone to come to her. She had a prickling sensation over her skin, as if something momentous was going to happen. And she couldn't forget the revelation that Rico had already known of her past. Perhaps not everything, but enough, and yet he'd wanted to wait for her to tell him. He hadn't used it against her.

It made her feel slightly panicky inside, with the sensation of no walls of defence left standing. What would happen now?

Gypsy dragged herself up and went to greet Lola, who said ecstatically, 'Mama!', and stood to greet her. Gypsy took her out and held her close, breathing in her delicious scent and feeling her solid weight. But already Lola was squirming to get down and be off exploring.

It was only when she was escaping out through the bedroom door that Gypsy realised she was looking for Rico, who appeared at that moment, cleanshaven and gorgeous in jeans and a T-shirt, and swung Lola up in his arms, much to her delight.

He looked at Gypsy, no discernible expression on his face. 'I'll take her down if you want to get dressed.'

So we can talk.

He didn't say it, but he didn't have to. He now had all the knowledge, all the power. Gypsy hated the way she automatically imagined the worst, but she'd had years of dealing with exactly that.

A short while later, dressed equally casually in jeans and a long-sleeved top, Gypsy joined the mayhem that was Lola's breakfast-time. Agneta was there too, cooing at Lola, who was happily holding court. Gypsy came in and had some coffee and a croissant, but she couldn't swallow past the huge lump in her throat.

When Agneta took Lola off, insisting that she would get her changed and dressed, Rico finally put down his napkin and stood.

'Will you come into my study?'

Gypsy looked up, and something dark made her say, 'Oh, so you're *asking* now?'

It was a mistake, because Rico glowered and all Gypsy could think of was the frantic coupling that had happened between them in there. With warmth suffusing her cheeks, she followed Rico.

Once in the study, Rico turned around to face Gypsy. Instinctively wanting to protect herself, she crossed her arms. Rico hitched one hip on the edge of his desk, and Gypsy fought not to let her gaze drop wantonly to where his jeans stretched over hard thighs.

'I had no idea you went through so much at the hands of that man.'

Gypsy looked at Rico before glancing away. His gaze was so intense. She shrugged. 'How could you have known? No one knew except for me.'

'That's why you didn't want to tell me about Lola, isn't it?'

Gypsy swallowed painfully. Her gaze swung back. 'It was a large part of it, yes. But, no matter what you believe, I *did* intend telling you. I just wanted to be in a better position…so you wouldn't see me as weak…and the thought of being dragged through the courts to prove paternity *was* daunting. I didn't want people finding out that I had been Alexandra Bastion and wondering where the family fortune had gone. I had never imagined that I might become pregnant. I truly did believe I'd be safe.'

Rico winced. 'I told you about that court case.

It was just unbelievably bad timing for you to have seen it that very morning.'

Rico stood from the desk and started to pace, making Gypsy's pulse race. She crossed her arms tighter across her chest.

He stopped to face her and in an uncharacteristically impatient gesture ran a hand through his hair. 'Look,' he began, 'it's clear now that we both had our reasons for reacting the way we did—you in your decision to keep Lola to yourself, and me for wanting her with me from the moment I knew about her.' He shook his head. 'I thought you were just like my mother—wilfully keeping me from Lola just because it served your purposes. And the thought of Lola possibly being brought up by some other man some day…enduring what I had…was too much to contemplate.'

Gypsy balked at the thought of *another man*. There would be no other man. Not ever. Not any more.

She bit her lip and said quietly, as that assertion rocked through her, 'I was just so terrified that you would be like my father…*worse*…because you were even more powerful than him. All I ever was was an inconvenient pawn to him.' She looked at Rico. 'I thought you would sweep in and take us over, remove me permanently from Lola's life the way my father did my mother.'

Rico shook his head. 'I was angry, yes, but I never thought of taking you away from Lola. I will admit that I saw a future where Lola was in my life and you were sidelined…but I don't see that future any more.'

'You don't?'

He shook his head. 'No.' His voice was a little gruff. 'I see a future with all of us together. I don't want this to end in fifteen months. I don't want to let you and Lola go. I want more than that, Gypsy. I want us to be a family…'

Gypsy started to tremble from her feet up. What Rico was saying was so huge. Massive. He wanted them to stay together. For ever? It was all at once the most exhilarating thing and the most terrifying. And in the midst of it all was her bone-deep ingrained fear and panic.

That snide voice was reminding her that men like Rico were masters of getting what they wanted. That he *had* swept in and taken them over. Look at them now—living on an island, effectively cut off from everything and everyone. And she had no idea how Rico really felt about her. He might be able to forgive her now, but what if that resentment was still there, buried and festering away? What if his desire waned and he wanted another woman?

Gypsy shook her head and started to back away, noticing the flash of Rico's eyes. He stood up straight at the desk, and his quick anger at her less than compliant response seemed to add fuel to her reasoning.

'You want me to agree to your plans just like that?' She snapped her fingers. 'You've been in our lives for a month, Rico, and suddenly you think that we can be a *family*?'

His frame bristled with energy. His jaw was tight. 'You're just saying that because it's hard for you to trust me.'

'Don't patronise me, Rico. From the word go you've stormed in and had it all your own way. This is exactly what I was afraid of.'

'Gypsy—' he sounded frustrated now '—you're not being rational.'

Something deep within Gypsy was surging up—something that had been buried for a long time. 'I am *not* my mother, Rico. I am not mentally weak. I have skills. I can take care of myself and my daughter.'

'I'm not saying you can't. What I'm saying is that I want to be there too. I want us to be together.'

'Because you want to control us.' Gypsy knew now that she was being irrational, but she couldn't stop.

'*No!* Dammit, Gypsy, no. Not because I want

to control you but because I love Lola. I don't
want to be separated from her and I—' He
stopped abruptly, concern etched on his face.
'What? What is it?'

He even came towards her, but she waved
him back—if he touched her now... For a heart-
stopping moment she'd thought he was about to
say he loved *her*, and when he hadn't...she'd felt
like collapsing. Of course he loved Lola. And he
wanted to do what was best for her. A million
miles from her own father. Suddenly Gypsy felt
ashamed.

Rico's voice was tight. 'Look, what is it going
to take for me to prove that you can trust me
and that I'm not like your father?'

Gypsy lifted stinging eyes to Rico and, with a
guilt that nearly crippled her, said the one thing
she wanted least. But she couldn't stop it—as
if on some level she thought if he could prove
this then she would gladly give him everything,
even if he didn't love her.

'I want to know that you will let us go if we
want to—that you won't cut yourself off from
Lola just to punish me.'

With his features pale and stark, Rico said
nothing for a long moment, and then he walked
out of the study. Before Gypsy could wonder
what he was doing he came back and held out
a key. She saw that it was the key to the Jeep.

'Go on—take it. I've instructed Agneta to pack up some things.'

Numbly Gypsy took the key and looked up into Rico's eyes. They were a cool slaty grey. 'You're just going to let us go? Right now? Like this?'

His mouth was a thin line. 'That's what you want, isn't it? That's what it's going to take?'

Suspecting he was just proving a point, but feeling utterly confused and bewildered, and thinking that perhaps even Rico had had enough by now, Gypsy nodded dumbly. She'd meant that she wanted him to assure her that he would let them go *if she wanted*, but now she realised that she might not have trusted that either. And through all of that was the heart-searing realisation that he *could* let her walk away—because she meant nothing to him.

Things happened quickly, and through it all a numbness settled over Gypsy as bags were put in the boot of the Jeep and as she strapped a bemused Lola into her chair. Poor Agneta was looking on, wringing her hands as if she had done something wrong.

Rico stood back. The only thing he said was, 'This doesn't mean you're out of my life. Lola will always know I'm here.'

Gypsy got into the Jeep and held herself together as she started it up with a shaking hand.

She had no earthly idea what to do or where to go. She was proving her point, and it was a disaster. But she drove out of the villa anyway, and set off along the coast road.

Almost immediately a plaintive wail came from the back of the Jeep. 'Papa!'

In her shock, Gypsy nearly swerved. Hearing Lola call Rico *Papa* for the first time, as if she'd just made the connection now that they were leaving, undid her completely. She had to pull over to a layby because her eyes were so blurred with tears.

And then Lola was wailing in earnest at Gypsy's distress.

The two of them were sitting there sobbing when suddenly Gypsy's door was wrenched open and Rico stood there, demanding, 'What is it? Did you crash? What's wrong?'

But Gypsy couldn't get a word out. She was crying too hard, even though Lola's wails had stopped and she was saying tearfully from the back, 'Papa... Papa...'

Rico took his attention to Lola and said wonderingly, 'She just called me Papa...' And then, soothingly, 'Everything is OK, *mi pequeña*—do you want to go home?'

Clearly Lola did something to indicate the affirmative, because then Rico was lifting Gypsy expertly into the passenger seat and suddenly they were turning around and driving back to the villa.

Through a blur of tears Gypsy saw Rico take Lola out and kiss her, before handing her to a relieved-looking Agneta, saying something in Greek which had Agneta nodding and smiling. And then he was at her door and lifting her out before she could protest. In all honesty Gypsy felt as weak as a rag doll.

Rico took her straight up to his bedroom and sat down on a chair in the corner with her on his lap. Gypsy was still sniffing and taking big convulsive breaths. Wordlessly Rico handed her a hanky, and she blew her nose loudly.

When she was more composed, and becoming very aware of sitting on Rico's steel-hard thighs, she tensed.

'Now...' he said. 'Do you believe that I'll let you go if you want to?'

Gypsy's heart beat fast. She looked at him suspiciously. 'You weren't far behind us.'

'Answer the question, Gypsy Butler. Do you believe that if you really want it, I'll let you go?'

Slowly she nodded her head, because she *did* believe it. In all honesty she'd believed it even before he'd orchestrated his little enactment.

He said now, 'I was following just to see that you were OK. You looked shell-shocked—I was worried. And,' he added, 'it's good that you believe me, because I'm never going to let you go again.'

Gypsy couldn't even gasp or act affronted. She just felt sadness well upwards. Tears formed again. She felt him tense, as if expecting a fight, and rushed to explain. 'It's not that I want to leave, I don't. But I don't see how loving Lola is going to make you happy in the long run— won't you want to meet someone else and settle down?'

Gypsy waved a shaking hand, not letting Rico speak. The tears were back, constricting her voice. 'I mean, Lola adores you, and you adore Lola, and it's the best thing I've ever seen, and I know now that you would never hurt her like my father did me…' She gulped in a breath. 'But it's going to get awfully embarrassing because…' Her heart thumped hard once, and then it spilled out. 'Because you see I adore you too, and I don't ever want you to send me away, and I *do* trust you, but it's scary because I've never trusted anyone, so I didn't believe it, and you won't thank me for these feelings when you want to move on…'

Rico shifted so that Gypsy fell into the cradle of his lap. He brought his hands to her face and wiped away the tears, and said gently, 'Can you stop talking and crying for one minute?'

There was such warmth in his voice that it shocked Gypsy's tears into stopping. She hic-cupped once. And blushed when she could feel the press of his arousal against her bottom. How could either of them be thinking of *that* at a time like this?

'Gypsy Butler...' Rico began, making sure she wasn't looking anywhere but into his eyes, which *glowed*, making her heart beat fast. 'Can you not tell how deeply and irrevocably in love with you I am?'

Wordlessly, shock hitting her, she just shook her head.

'Well, I am. I was about to tell you earlier, but then you looked as if you were going to faint. I started falling for you when I saw you in the club that night. I was ready to walk out, bored beyond tears, cursing myself for having gone in at all—and then you walked in, and I couldn't look away. You looked so wild and free and totally different to anyone else.'

His thumbs stroked her cheeks, and Gypsy could feel herself leaning against him, melting all over.

'And then...that night...it was magical. I felt like I'd met the one person who connected with the real *me*. Not the tycoon. And I was such a fool to leave you like that in the morning, but I was freaked out by how much you'd made me feel: possessive, and yearning for something I'd never even noticed I wanted before...'

'It was like that for me too,' Gypsy said, feeling shy, still not really believing she was hearing this.

'And then you were gone, and all I knew was that I'd spent the night with a temptress called Gypsy and I didn't even think that was your real name. For the past two years you've haunted my dreams and my life. I tried to recreate what I experienced with you but it never happened. I was growing increasingly cynical and delusional and then I saw you again. I thought I was dreaming you up.'

'But...just now...you let me walk away...'

An intense light lit his eyes. 'To be honest I didn't think you'd go through with it. But then I realised I had to let you go, or else you never would have trusted that I *could* let you go. You and Lola mean everything to me, but if you're not happy here then I would never keep you against your will. I have to warn you, though, I'll follow you wherever you go...'

He drew her head down to his and started to kiss her, as delicately and tenderly as if she were made of fine bone china. Impatient with his restraint, Gypsy deepened the kiss, her tongue stroking erotically along Rico's until she heard him groan and finally he gave in to his passion.

She was being lifted from the chair, and suddenly they were tumbling onto Rico's bed and his hands were everywhere, desire rising to fever-pitch as they both struggled to be free of conflicting clothes, needing to forge a deeper union.

Finally, blissfully naked, Gypsy arched her whole body against Rico's hard physique and revelled in his indrawn breath. He pressed her down and moved over her, both hands framing her face, her hair spilling out around her head.

He looked down at her, and nothing but love shone from his eyes.

'There's just one other thing.'

For a second something familiarly panicky skated over Gypsy's skin, and she asked warily, 'What?'

He waited for a moment, a wicked glint in his eyes. And then said finally, 'If it's not too scary a prospect, and if I promise not to ever control you but to give you all the freedom you want, will you trust me enough to marry me, Gypsy Butler?'

Love and passion infused every cell, and she felt the final release of all her old fears. She smiled up at Rico tremulously and reached up to caress his jaw. 'I trust you with all my heart, and our daughter's life. And I'd love to marry you.'

Rico saw the tears forming in her eyes and started to kiss her again, moving over her body so that she could feel his hardness. He growled mock-seriously, 'No more tears. I won't allow it. Only smiles and laughter from now on…and love.'

He joined their bodies, and Gypsy gasped at the exquisite sensation, too distracted to think about crying any more even if they were happy tears.

EPILOGUE

LOLA handed Rico's phone back to him and lisped through her two missing front teeth, 'There you go, Daddy, now you have the *newest* newest ringtone.'

Rico repressed a grimace when he thought of the effect the last ringtone had had on a recent high-powered meeting, and said, while holding back a wry smile, 'Thanks, Lola, I wasn't so sure about that last one.'

Lola flung her arms around Rico's neck and gave him a quick sloppy kiss, 'You'll love this one. It's *really* loud so you'll always hear when we're calling you.'

Rico shook his head indulgently and watched as she sped off to play with Agneta's grand-son, from whom she was inseparable, her hair bouncing with wild and curly disarray around her shoulders.

Just then Gypsy appeared, wearing a short sundress that did nothing to conceal her gorgeous body and everything to send Rico's pulse-rate soaring. Her hair was only slightly less wild than their daughter's, with long tendrils curling over bare sun-kissed skin.

She led a small endearingly grumpy-looking boy by the hand; Zack had obviously woken prematurely from his nap, and Rico opened his arms so that he could clamber up and snuggle into his chest, promptly falling asleep again with a thumb stuck firmly into his mouth, exactly as his older sister had used to do.

Rico pulled Gypsy gently down beside him on the family lounger. She leant in to give him a long, lingering kiss. When they broke apart he caressed her jaw, rubbing her bottom lip with his thumb, and sighed with obvious but good-humoured frustration. The look that zinged between them said it all.

Gypsy smiled ruefully and put a hand on her swollen belly. 'I'd forgotten that I can never seem to nap when I'm pregnant...'

Rico smiled too, and growled softly, 'In which case we should aim for a nice early bedtime tonight...it's been far too long since I felt your naked body against mine, Mrs Christofides.'

Gypsy blushed to think of how they'd woken so entwined that morning. Rico had only had to make a subtle movement to bring them into more intimate contact. It had been slow and unbearably sensual. Full of love. She smiled. 'You're insatiable.'

'Only for you, *mi amor.*' Rico smiled, his eyes tender on his wife's face, revelling in the oceans of love that surrounded them. 'Only for you.'

LARGER-PRINT BOOKS!

 HARLEQUIN *Presents*

PASSION GUARANTEED SEDUCTION

GET 2 FREE LARGER-PRINT
NOVELS PLUS 2 FREE GIFTS!

YES! Please send me 2 FREE LARGER-PRINT Harlequin Presents® novels and my 2 FREE gifts (gifts are worth about $10). After receiving them, if I don't wish to receive any more books, I can return the shipping statement marked "cancel". If I don't cancel, I will receive 6 brand-new novels every month and be billed just $4.55 per book in the U.S. or $5.24 per book in Canada. That's a saving of at least 13% off the cover price! It's quite a bargain! Shipping and handling is just 50¢ per book.* I understand that accepting the 2 free books and gifts places me under no obligation to buy anything. I can always return a shipment and cancel at any time. Even if I never buy another book, the two free books and gifts are mine to keep forever.

176/376 HDN E5NG

Name _____ (PLEASE PRINT)

Address _____ Apt. #

City _____ State/Prov. _____ Zip/Postal Code

Signature (if under 18, a parent or guardian must sign)

Mail to the **Harlequin Reader Service:**
IN U.S.A.: P.O. Box 1867, Buffalo, NY 14240-1867
IN CANADA: P.O. Box 609, Fort Erie, Ontario L2A 5X3

Not valid for current subscribers to Harlequin Presents Larger-Print books.

**Are you a subscriber to Harlequin Presents books
and want to receive the larger-print edition?
Call 1-800-873-8635 today!**

* Terms and prices subject to change without notice. Prices do not include applicable taxes. Sales tax applicable in N.Y. Canadian residents will be charged applicable provincial taxes and GST. Offer not valid in Quebec. This offer is limited to one order per household. All orders subject to approval. Credit or debit balances in a customer's account(s) may be offset by any other outstanding balance owed by or to the customer. Please allow 4 to 6 weeks for delivery. Offer available while quantities last.

Your Privacy: Harlequin Books is committed to protecting your privacy. Our Privacy Policy is available online at www.eHarlequin.com or upon request from the Reader Service. From time to time we make our lists of customers available to reputable third parties who may have a product or service of interest to you. If you would prefer we not share your name and address, please check here. ☐

Help us get it right—We strive for accurate, respectful and relevant communications. To clarify or modify your communication preferences, visit us at www.ReaderService.com/consumerschoice.

HPLP10R

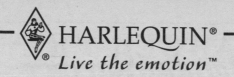